second encounter

First published in Bengali as
Je Jekhane Danriye by Ananda Publishers in 1972.

Published by
NIYOGI BOOKS
D-78, Okhla Industrial Area, Phase-I
New Delhi-110 020, INDIA
Tel: 91-11-26816301, 49327000
Fax: 91-11-26810483, 26813830
email: niyogibooks@gmail.com
website: www.niyogibooksindia.com

Editor: Upama Biswas
Cover Design: Misha Oberoi

ISBN: 978-93-85285-44-8
Publication: 2016

This is a work of fiction. The names, characters and incidents portrayed in it are the work of the author's imagination. Any resemblance to actual persons, living or dead, events or localities, is entirely coincidental.

Printed at: Niyogi Offset Pvt. Ltd., New Delhi, India

second encounter

ramapada chowdhury

TRANSLATED FROM THE BENGALI NOVELLA *JE JEKHANE DANRIYE*
BY SWAPNA DUTTA

NIYOGI BOOKS

Chapter 1

SUNLIGHT streamed into the rectangular veranda at the back of the guest house where Anupam sat huddled in a cane chair with his feet up. Beyond the veranda there was a low courtyard. Anupam detested the cold and enjoyed being out in the sun. More so, because he was not getting any younger! But the chilly weather did not seem to trouble Anita in the least. Anupam was not sure whether women in general felt the cold less or if they merely pretended that they did for the sake of bravado.

"Don't you think it is colder than usual this year, Anu?" he had asked her a little while ago and she had instantly replied, "No, it isn't. It's you who is getting old, my dear!"

Anupam had not found her words amusing. Age was no respecter of persons. Wasn't Anita getting older too? She said it simply because she had now moved over to her son's camp and, like him, she too did not find this place attractive any more. But unlike them Anupam felt a strong craving to escape here whenever he was free from college. He loved the tranquillity of the place and the feeling of being totally free from all hassles. Fortunately, not many people were aware of the existence of Musabani Haludpukur. Even if they had been, there was little chance of their piling on here because the place was not meant for casual trips and there were very few places to stay.

Anupam enjoyed the eerie, romantic feeling that got hold of him whenever he walked towards the Rakha Mines. The entire area was full of trees that seemed to have come up at random. In between the trees stood broken, mossy walls, nearly two-storeys high, standing on their own like ruins of some ancient city. Long ago, during the heydays of this region, the district used to be full of large houses that had sprung up all around the copper mines. But when the mining company failed and finally closed shop, the empty dwellings perished at the hands of Time. Only parts of their boundary walls that were as high as prison embankments remained intact.

In fact, Musabani was totally unlike any city Anupam had come across and had a charm of its own. There was a distinct tang of minerals in the air. Kainite stones with streaks of white and green were strewn all around. Buckets carrying copper ore, rock phosphate, asbestos and quartzite swished along the high ropeways overhead. One could see the Shurgi Hill at a distance and the Sankh River flowing way down below. The entire region was cloaked in the shadow of the green woods surrounding the place. It was hardly surprising that people from the city would find the place attractive. Anupam felt that he was on a real holiday, free from the cares of the entire busy world, whenever he came to stay in this guest house. His life, which mostly consisted of delivering the same lectures year after year to a changing group of students, felt distinctly stale, bland and monotonous at times. But whenever he came here his entire being was recharged and the missing colours of life crept in once again.

An ex-student of Anupam had started a country liquor distillery in this district. It soon became necessary for him to build a guest house as well for the sake of business. This student—a young Muslim boy—held him in great respect and refused to take any payment for his stay. It was mainly because of him that Anupam visited the place with his family every now and then.

But Musabani had its own problems. The most important one was the inordinate delay in getting the daily newspaper. It never reached Anupam before eleven, even at the earliest. And this meant there was nothing to do until then. He found it a problem to fill up this blank period of inactivity. Of course, as always, he had not failed to carry his bundle of examination papers that had to be checked and marked. But he did not even feel like touching the bundle!

Normally Anupam enjoyed a second cup of tea around this time and went out for a walk. But he had caught a chill the previous day. As a result, he simply sat in the veranda enjoying the warmth of the winter sun. Sipping his second cup of tea with a shawl around his torso had a charm of its own and was far more desirable than trudging along the uneven path outside. Had it been the day for the weekly local market, Anita would have been after him by now, pestering him and insisting on his going there. She would have reminded him repeatedly how important it was to fetch things from the market and then end up losing her temper. "Mark my words, you are not going to have any lunch before two this afternoon," she would announce angrily. Fortunately today was not the market day. So he could rest here in peace. And yet, he would have been very happy if it had been. This morning, his thoughts lingered on the market as he re-lived those special moments when he was there last evening, over and over again.

A rooster just outside the veranda was trying to get inside the courtyard with frisky steps, shaking its combed head. It strutted like a hero in a play and was least bothered by Anupam's shouts. But his yell scared the hen and its newborn chicks and they tried to run out of the courtyard. Anupam put down his cup of tea and called out, "Bappa! Hasu!"

No one answered.

Comfortably seated and well wrapped up, Anupam didn't feel like getting up himself. He raised his voice and called Bappa once again. But it was Anita who came instead.

"Why are you calling Bappa?" she asked, "He is in a real bad mood right now."

"What on earth for?" asked Anupam, surprised.

"Obviously because he doesn't like being here," answered Anita.

Her words explained why Bappa had been going about with a glum face for the last few days. Anupam could not understand the boy's sudden craving for Calcutta. Was it because he had just joined college and was missing his new friends?

"But this is such a beautiful place…all these woodlands and…" said Anupam, looking surprised.

Anita laughed. "You are getting old. That's why you find this remote, out-of-beyond place attractive. But don't forget that poor Bappa is only eighteen!"

Anupam had never minded being reminded that he was getting old in the past. On the contrary, he had found the statement rather amusing. But after what happened at the market last evening he felt a sudden craving to turn young once again. That was why he did not find Anita's remark funny this morning and could not laugh it off as usual. Anita was walking away, barely supressing a chuckle, when she noticed the frown on Anupam's face and stopped short. She brought her head close to his face and said, "Look at me, dear sir. I've got a grey hair too! Which means, it's high time I too turned serious like you."

Anupam looked at the strand of grey hair and said, "So you have a grey hair too! You've been hiding it all this time? Or have you been plucking them off on the sly?"

His words made Anita angry. "If I had done that I wouldn't have bothered to show you this one."

Anupam burst out laughing at her reaction and called out to his children, "Hey Bappa! Hasu! Just see what's happened..." Anita did not approve of this kind of jokes in the presence of her eighteen-year-old son. She frowned at Anupam and was about to leave the place when Bappa came running, looking flustered. "Baba..." he said breathlessly, "Baba, there's a gentleman come to see you. And there's a lady with him."

Anupam jumped up. "To see me? Where are they?"

Bappa had always been restless by nature. He had shot up in height and was nearly as tall as Anupam now. Whenever he walked, his long strides made it seem as though he was running. When they went out together, Anupam could barely keep pace with him these days. Bappa made a dash for the gate, suddenly remembering that he ought to have taken the visitors to the drawing room and asked them to be seated before calling his father. A foolish slip on his part!

Anupam's eyes rested on the lady before anyone else. He suddenly felt strangely elated. It was something he had never imagined in his wildest of dreams. But he also felt slightly uncomfortable. Then he looked at the gentleman who was walking towards them. Anupam had not found it difficult to recognise the lady and this knowledge made him feel both ashamed and embarrassed. Because thereby hung the tale of a wound that lay deep down within his heart.

"I don't think you recognised me at the weekly market last evening," said the lady in a voice that held accusation as well as a touch of embarrassment. She looked self-conscious despite her attempt to appear natural.

Anupam tried not to show the tingling sensation he felt all over his body.

The gentleman laughed at his wife's words and said, "In that case, ask him now, if he remembers you!"

Anupam managed to control his feelings and assume a casual air as he replied, "I did think for a moment that it was you. But I couldn't be sure as I was not wearing my glasses. My distant vision isn't too good these days."

Turning towards the house, he said, "Please come in."

"No. You must first tell me who I am."

As though he had not known her the moment he saw her! As if she could ever be a stranger to him! Anupam laughed at her words.

"You are Anjali, of course."

"So, you *do* remember me?" Anjali smiled at him. "But I got the distinct feeling that you did not because you simply looked the other way last evening."

"In that case, why didn't you speak to him first?" asked her husband with a smile, "Why blame him alone?" Anupam returned the smile. They were in the drawing room now. Anjali's husband introduced himself, adding, "I am a geologist. I am here for a few months on a field job."

Anupam looked back and saw Hasu standing at the door, looking at Anjali curiously.

"This is my daughter," Anupam told his guests. Then he looked at her and said, "Hasu, go and call your mother." Finally he looked at Bappa and said, "This is Bappa, my elder son. The younger one did not come with us. He chose to stay back at his uncle's place."

Anjali had been looking around. "It's a lovely house," she remarked.

Anupam smiled, looking deep into her eyes, and said, "Please be seated. I'll be right back."

He went to the kitchen with rapid steps and found Anita, Bappa and Hasu discussing about the unexpected guests in a low voice. He heard Hasu telling her mother excitedly, "The lady looks so sweet, Maa. Who is she?"

Anita, casually dressed in a simple sari, was in the middle of cooking lunch, her hands smeared with turmeric. She felt annoyed at this sudden intrusion and asked her husband, "Who is it? One of your students?"

"Oh no," said Anupam, laughing, "Do you remember my telling you that we used to live in Simla Street when I was young? This lady used to be our neighbour. She was Bilu's friend, actually."

Bilu was Anupam's younger brother.

Anita made a face as she said, "I can't imagine why people choose to call at such odd hours, just when one is busy."

She was about to go out and change into a better sari when Anjali herself came into the kitchen.

"It is you I have come to meet," said Anjali to Anita in a voice full of laughter, "and you've been keeping out of my sight all this time."

She put her arms round Hasu and said, "What a nice, quiet girl you have! My daughter is a regular tomboy."

Anjali inspected the kitchen, courtyard, the corridor and even their bedroom. She praised the curtains on the window and touched the bedspread, saying, "What a pretty design!"

Anita's feeling of discomfort vanished in a moment. Anjali seemed just like an old friend. But Anupam still felt that there was a rigid wall between himself and Anjali and could not bring himself to talk to her naturally. He sat chatting with Anjali's geologist husband instead and listened to Anjali's words and laughter floating in from the other room. A wave of delight swept through his heart that seemed to whisper, *Anjali is here…Anjali is really here…*

Anupam had been to the weekly market the previous evening along with his local maid, a Santhal (belonging to the Santhal tribe) girl named Budhli. He always enjoyed going around the market, not just to buy things like fish, meat and vegetables but also to look at the various stalls set out there. Some of them decorated their temporary stall with handwoven thread, locally dyed, laying them down in bunches on the muddy floor. Others had piles of beads in varied colours—necklaces, copper armlets and silver-coated brass ornaments. A crowd of Santhal girls flocked to the shop of Mewalal, the one-armed moneylender, who sold mill-made saris, dresses made of coarse jute flannel and prickly rugs. Some stalls displayed thick, loom-woven saris and sheets along with crudely made shirts and blouses. As this was pay-day in the mines most of the buyers were coolies. There was a man selling *bindis* made from the glossy wings of *kanchpoka*, scorpion oil and many such strange concoctions. Many of the young girls held each other by the waist as they laughed and joked amongst themselves.

There were vegetable stalls on the other side of the market selling ridge gourd, brinjal and tomatoes. Nearly every stall had chicken tied up with strings. Anupam had been picking up things at random when his eyes fell on the distant track where a lady was approaching the market. It was not unusual to come across a city girl or two at the local market. But there was no mistaking Anjali's tall and graceful figure that stood out from the others. She soon got busy shopping, a pretty, embroidered bag in her hand. After paying for the ridge gourds that she had picked up she looked up suddenly. As her eyes met Anupam's, a wave of thrill swept through him. The utter surprise of confronting her also carried a touch of pain which was inexplicable. The pain wrung his heart the moment he saw Anjali. Yes, he could feel it plainly, deep inside his heart, even after all these years!

Anupam could hardly believe his luck at first. But strangely enough, he was too flustered to look into Anjali's eyes and looked the other way. He completed his own shopping and returned home as fast as possible without giving her a second glance. But his heart continued to hover around the market place. Wasn't it strange that he should meet her here, in this quiet, out-of-the-way place, when both of them lived in Calcutta? But although he felt elated at seeing her, he could not get over his feeling of deep hurt nurtured over the years. He had not imagined for a moment that Anjali herself would come to his guest house to find him!

When the visitors stood up to leave, Anupam looked at Anjali with steady eyes. But this time it was Anjali who looked the other way. But in that single moment her eyes flashed a world of unspoken messages. Anupam looked at her once again. She was as tall and graceful as ever. Perhaps she was a trifle slimmer when he knew her before. But now her obvious sense of security and contentment with life made her seem even more beautiful. Her eyes spelt peace within. Anupam and Bappa also walked with them part of the way to see them off. As they sauntered along, Anupam heard Anjali's geologist husband speaking to Bappa, telling him about the local stones. Picking up a piece of rock, he pointed out its features to Bappa, "Look at this rock with golden streaks, Bappa. It is copper pyrite. The golden lines are all copper." Anjali heard her husband holding forth on his favourite subject and smiled at Anupam. As they walked side by side she suddenly said, "You don't see distant things very clearly, isn't that so?"

Anupam remembered that this was the excuse he himself had given her for not speaking to her last evening. Her words seemed to drench his entire being like an invisible fountain of joy. He replied, "Believe me, Anjali, I was too scared to speak to you."

Anjali's voice grew intense with emotion as she whispered, "Didn't we spend our entire lifetime just being afraid?"

They walked on in silence. Suddenly Anjali said, "It's been so long…so very long…full twenty years!"

Anupam echoed her words, "Twenty years!" He sighed and tried to smile. "Who would believe us if we told them that this is the first time that we are actually speaking to each other?"

Anjali replied in a voice muffled with tears, "But I have been speaking to you within my heart for the last twenty years!"

Chapter 2

ALTHOUGH no one was aware of the earthquake that had suddenly taken place within Anupam's heart, Anjali's visit had managed to create ripples in the entire household, just as a pebble thrown into a still pond does. Anupam liked Ranen, Anjali's geologist husband, who seemed devoted to her. Besides, he seemed to be modest, well-mannered and of a cool temperament. His head office was located in Calcutta but the company owned some mines here and Ranen was here to inspect how the local work was progressing. Anupam had often seen the house where they stayed on his way to the market.

As they walked, Ranen stopped suddenly and folded his hands, saying, "You'd better go back now, Anupam babu, or else *we'll* have to see you home." Then he burst out laughing at his own joke. Anupam and Bappa stopped walking. But instead of turning back, Anupam continued to stand there shamelessly even after he saw Ranen and Anjali walking back together, deep in some discussion. Anjali looked back suddenly. Her tragic eyes seemed to send him a silent message that wrung his heart with pain. Even at this age!

Perhaps he had forgotten all about Anjali. Had they not met so unexpectedly or spoken to each other after all these years, he would never have known how carefully he had preserved her memories deep within his heart. He glanced at Bappa after the look that passed between Anjali and himself. Suddenly he seemed to discover his own young self in his son, full of the same innocence and purity of youth. He had wanted to stop and tell her: *Anjali, you are still as precious and sacred to me as the scriptures. The language of your eyes turn my feelings into a mantra.*

Anupam and Bappa walked back the rest of the way in silence. Anupam did not feel like breaking the spell by talking. But a wave of regret swept over him for not having spoken to Anjali before when he had met her so suddenly. There was so much that he wanted to tell her! And so much that he longed to know about her! His inner self whispered: *Anjali, where you are concerned, my heart is still eighteen and as you know, desire has no age.*

He seemed to feel the intensity in Anjali's voice once again as her words kept ringing in his ears: *After so long…so very long…twenty years!*

Anupam wanted to be on his own after returning home so that he might dive into the pool of memories. But everyone else wanted to talk about Anjali and Ranen.

"Really, Dada, you are the absolute limit!" said Hasu, "Why didn't you take me along with you when you went to see them off? I liked aunty very much! She is so jolly!"

"I liked Ranen babu immensely," said Anita as she wiped her wet hands in her *anchal*, "he is such a simple and unpretentious gentleman."

"He is quite serious-minded," said Bappa, interrupting his mother, "he was telling me so many interesting facts about minerals."

"Shut up," said Hasu, "you can only talk about studies and drag general knowledge into everything."

Anupam felt gratified to see that Anjali's visit had caused quite a stir within his quiet family. Apparently she had also managed to charm everyone at the same time. But his delight was tinged with regret. It seemed to him that the young girl he had perceived with his eighteen-year-old eyes was with him still, following him wherever he went. How old would Anjali be right now? He tried to calculate it mentally. Not more than thirty-six or thirty-seven. But although the thirty-six-year-old Anjali had left his house after her visit she had left behind the seventeen-year-old girl who had been part of his youth.

Anupam always enjoyed his afternoon siesta after lunch when sunlight streamed into his bedroom touching the bed with its warm glow. There was nothing cosier than feeling the sun on his back on a chilly winter noon. But that afternoon Anupam could not sleep as usual because he did not want to. He had meant to tackle the unmarked answer papers. But he did not feel like touching those either. Despite his intention of checking them during this vacation, he hadn't even got as far as untying the bundle. All his joy seemed to evaporate whenever he thought of those unmarked examination papers! The thought that he had not looked at them pricked him like a thorn and kept reminding him that he would have to get down to it sooner or later. But it was a distasteful prospect.

Now that Anjali had grabbed all his attention, he had no time for anything else.

He closed his eyes and re-lived every moment of that fateful evening once again. He felt like rushing back to Anjali and telling her: *I remember everything about our past. Every single thing. Nothing is lost, not even a single moment of anything related to you.*

He got off the bed, finally, with a mixed feeling of joy and excitement. He turned back to find Anita, Bappa and Hasu fast asleep. But there was no siesta for Anupam that afternoon.

Anupam went out of the room, opened the main door and stood looking at the horizon. He could see the Shurgi Hill and the woods surrounding it and the rough and uneven paths leading to it. He saw the clear sky up above and the Sankh River far away. He remembered walking that way during one of his previous visits and recalled the neat and tidy mud houses standing in a cluster in the little Santhal village, their smooth mud walls painted a slate grey, yellow or saffron. Some of the walls had pictures on them. He could not see the houses from this distance but the view itself was soothing to the eyes. He could also see a group of Santhal girls walking slowly, carrying mud pitchers on their heads. Somehow the locality itself seemed to have been transformed for him, acquiring a fresh, new colour. Anupam gazed at the scene fascinated. Just then he heard someone calling. It was the voice of a young girl calling out to someone in a melodious voice. Anupam pricked up his ears and tried to catch the name. Then he clearly heard someone calling out to Bappa.

"Bap-pa...Bap-pa..."

Anupam called Bappa as soon as he heard the name clearly. Then he came and stood outside the door. He heard the voice calling once again—"Bap-pa!"

Anupam tried to see who it was but could see no one.

Bappa was up by then. He splashed some water on his face and made his way towards the garden. It was already quite late and the sun was about to set. The twilight was streaked with the shadow of the green forest in the distance. Anupam came to the balcony outside and looked about him. Then he caught sight of a young girl just outside the gate. She looked like a seventeen-year-old and was seated on a cycle with one foot balanced on the iron gate. She was dressed in a pair of black slacks and a loose, embroidered top, bright orange in colour. She was smiling, as though she found the situation vastly amusing. The rays of the setting sun combined with the orange of her top gave her pretty, fair face a radiant glow. Anupam thought she looked like a beautiful painting. The girl saw Bappa standing on the balcony but she continued to call him in her strange way—"Bap-pa…Bap-pa". Bappa looked at his father in surprise, not recognising the girl. Then he walked towards her and asked, "Were you calling *me* by any chance?"

The girl laughed and jumped down from her cycle. Then she placed it against the hedge and asked, "Are *you* Bappa?" Bappa was feeling annoyed at the way she had been calling out his name. He sounded unnecessarily grim as he replied, "Yes, I am."

The girl suddenly caught sight of Anupam and moved towards him, ignoring Bappa altogether. She touched Anupam's feet in salutation and said, "Uncle, I am Jhumjhum. I know my mother has told you that I'm a tomboy and that I'm a disobedient spoilt brat and all sorts of things when she came to visit you this morning. Please tell me, Uncle, what else did she tell you about me?" She laughed as she spoke. Anupam also burst out laughing at her words.

"So, you are Jhumjhum?" he asked. He had not found it difficult to recognise Anjali's daughter. She was a smart girl and seemed to have a sense of humour.

"Where do you study?" Anupam asked her.

Jhumjhum laughed again and replied, "Me? Oh well, I failed to clear my Higher Secondary this year."

Then she looked at Bappa and said, "I heard you got above 80 per cent in two subjects? Maa said so. In fact, she was praising you to the skies. Tell me, how did you manage to do it? You must be really good at copying!"

This time Bappa burst out laughing. Then he gave her a serious look and said, "I don't need to copy. I did well because I take my studies seriously."

"Don't tell me!" said Jhumjhum, pretending to be surprised, "I know that boys are particularly clever at copying from others.

Otherwise how do they manage to do get through the exams? It's quite impossible unless you're a copy-cat!"

Bappa normally kept his voice low before his father. But Jhumjhum's words made him see red as he replied, "But *you* failed in spite of copying, didn't you?"

Jhumjhum loved to tease and laughed loudly to see Bappa so angry. She said, "Very well then, have it your way! You are a goody-goody wonder and managed to clear your exams because you studied hard. Satisfied?"

Then she turned to Anupam and said, "Tell me, Uncle, don't you think that anyone who studies all the time is bound to pass? What's so surprising or unique about that?"

This time Anupam laughed at her. "Quite right," he said.

Anupam found Jhumjhum's words and attitude both amusing and attractive. She seemed like a breath of fresh air in a stuffy room. Or a streak of warm sunlight on a foggy winter morning. She was here in a strange house with completely unknown people and yet she was totally at ease.

Their conversation must have woken Anita. She too came out of her room, followed by sleepy-eyed Hasu who looked at Jhumjhum curiously.

Anupam introduced them. "This is Jhumjhum, Anjali's daughter."

"Really?" said Anita, drawing her close and placing her hand on her shoulder. "How could your mother describe such a pretty girl as a tomboy?"

"Just look at me, Aunty. Don't I look fairly harmless?" asked Jhumjhum, "Unfortunately, my mother is totally unable to discover anything good in me!"

Her gestures made her words sound absurdly funny. It was impossible not to laugh. But at the same time, her words did not fail to charm the listeners. The more she spoke, the more Anita laughed. Jhumjhum was totally unlike any other seventeen-year-old she had come across. Nor was her behaviour anything like the girls of her age with whom Anita was familiar. She had been compelled to buy her daughter the same kind of top and slacks last year because Hasu insisted on buying them. But she did not really like her wearing them. But the same clothes looked just right on Jhumjhum, perhaps because she was particularly attractive. Despite her smartness there was something homely and soothing about her personality.

Jhumjhum suddenly said, "I completely forgot to tell you my reason for coming here. All of you are invited to dinner at our place tonight." She burst out laughing once again.

Anupam felt uncomfortable when he heard of the sudden invitation. So did Anita, who said, "Why the hurry? We are not running away! We'll definitely come to your place some other day."

She was ready with several excuses. "Your uncle hasn't been feeling too well, you see." Then she added, "How could your mother send you here all alone? After all, you hadn't met any of us before."

Jhumjhum smiled and said, "It wasn't Maa who sent me here. Baba was coming to invite you. But I told him that I'd do it and would be able to locate your place quite easily. You see, I already knew your guest house. As a matter of fact, I know all the houses in this area."

Anita asked Jhumjhum to wait and fetched a plate of sweets for her. But Jhumjhum jumped up, saying, "I'd better not stay if you cancel the invitation. And I don't want any sweets either." But she had to pick up one because Anita insisted on her having it. She swallowed it the way one swallows a pill and said, "I can't go and tell them at home that you're not coming." She turned to Bappa and said, "Look here, Bappa, why don't you come with me and tell them yourself?"

Anupam also smiled at her words and said, “Yes, you’d better go with her, Bappa, and explain the situation to them.”

Bappa and Jhumjhum left the house together. Anupam noticed that Jhumjhum was riding the cycle very slowly to keep pace with Bappa’s steps. Anita also smiled.

As the two of them went out of sight along the bend in the road, Anita’s eyes fell on Hasu, who stood there looking bewildered.

“You too could have gone with them,” said Anita, looking at Hasu, “Why didn’t you?”

Chapter 3

A STRIP along the muddy uneven path had got flattened by people's footsteps. Those who rode cycles always stuck to that smoothened strip. But it had potholes too which compelled Jhumjhum to get off her cycle every now and then. Bappa walked while Jhumjhum rode beside him slowly, keeping pace with his steps. Bappa could not help admiring her ability to maintain balance at such slow speed. The road got worse as they walked further. Finally, Jhumjhum got off the cycle and stood waiting for Bappa to catch up. Giving him a naughty smile, she asked, "Has the good-goody wonder got over his anger yet?" Bappa had already forgotten her earlier comments. "What anger?" he asked, surprised.

"For saying that you had scored 80 per cent marks by copying from somebody else."

Both of them burst out laughing. The cloud of reserve vanished into thin air.

Bappa grabbed the handle of the cycle and said, "Let me ride a little."

"Dear me! Do you mean to say that you can actually ride a bicycle?" asked Jhumjhum, pretending to be surprised.

Bappa did not bother to reply. He walked across the next pothole and got on to the cycle.

"Mine is a ladies' bike, mind you. People are going to laugh if they see you riding it," warned Jhumjhum.

"Rubbish!" said Bappa, "It's you they'll laugh at, not me."

But he got off the cycle almost immediately and said, "I wish one could get cycles for hire at this place."

"Oh yes, that would be great," agreed Jhumjhum. "We could have gone off on long rides together if they did. People would be worried and Maa would possibly be in tears. But we could laugh at them on our return. Really, Bappa, should we try it some time?"

Bappa had his own ideas. He smiled at her and said, "What if we don't have cycles? We could take the bus from Haludpukur and…"

Jhumjhum, in love with her own voice, loved to hear herself speak. She did not hear Bappa's suggestion and cried, "Bappa, just see how lovely it is out there!"

Bappa looked up and was struck by the scene before him. The place was strewn with rocks of different sizes. The lonely hill stood at a distance with the clear blue sky above. The western sky had taken on the colour of liquid gold. The sun was about to set. Before long the sky was ablaze with the glow of the setting sun. Little fluffy clouds scattered in the sky reflected myriad hues. Neither Bappa nor Jhumjhum knew how or just when it happened. But right then the clouds looked like kites of different colours afloat in the sky—brown and golden, purple and blue. Bappa and Jhumjhum stood looking at the skyscape, enchanted. Jhumjhum said, "Look, Bappa, doesn't that blue cloud look like the face of a man?" Bappa said, "That golden cloud there looks like the map of India. Oh look! See how the shapes are changing." The coloured clouds were now moving fast as their shapes changed. The face of a man took on the shape of an elephant. The map of India became a dancing girl.

Bappa and Jhumjhum saw the evening light fading gradually as the shadow of darkness descended upon the treetops. The forest looked like an inky sea with dark waves breaking, one after the other. They stood looking for a long time and then walked a few steps, paused and looked again.

This time Bappa said "Lovely!" the way Jhumjhum had said it a few moments ago. Jhumjhum was lost in her own thoughts.

There was an elevated mound along the path with a huge tree just beside it, sending out thick roots on all sides. Jhumjhum looked at it and said, "Could we sit here for a while, Bappa? It's such an enchanted evening. I don't feel like leaving this place right now."

Bappa nodded silently. They sat on the thick roots, gazing at the sky above them. No one spoke. It seemed as though words would break the spell of wonder that surrounded them. Time moved on. A bullock cart trudged across, breaking the silence. Workers were already beginning to return home from the mines.

"Jhumjhum!" called Bappa softly.

Jhumjhum did not reply. She did not feel like talking. After a while she stood up as if suddenly awake. Bappa got up too. She pushed the cycle along, Bappa walking next to her.

"Bappa, don't you think I have a rotten name?" she asked suddenly.

Bappa smiled. Then he called her softly, "Hi Jhumjhumi!"

"Ugh! That sounds even worse!"

Bappa smiled again and said, "Jhumur-jhum then?"

Jhumjhum broke into unbridled laughter.

Bappa was also thinking deeply as they walked with the bicycle between them, Jhumjhum to the right and Bappa to the left. Bappa stretched his left hand and rang the bell twice to pull Jhumjhum out of her trance. When she failed to respond, Bappa called out, "Hi Khuku (little girl)!"

Jhumjhum halted immediately and looked at Bappa, amused. "How sweet that sounds! Believe me, no one has ever called me Khuku before." Her words and gestures made Bappa smile.

"Well, I'm not going to call you Khuku either," he said, "I'll give you another name."

He stopped and wondered what name he could give her.

"What name?" asked Jhumjhum, "Tell me immediately!"

"I don't really know what I'd call you," said Bappa slowly, "but I do feel like giving you a fresh name at this moment. I'll think about it and when I hit upon the correct one, I shall call you by that name."

Jhumjhum, who had been listening to Bappa with an amused face, said, "Good heavens! Are you really planning to think about me that long?" She paused for a moment and said, "But I am not going to think about you! I don't like to think about anything or anybody for long!"

"Then, what do you like to do?" asked Bappa curiously.

The sky along the horizon, visible through the branches of the trees, had already turned to grey from golden red. Jhumjhum looked at the fading sunlight and said, "I'd like someone to wait for me far away while I sit at home and think of his forlorn face. Then I'd laugh loudly thinking about it and when my mother would ask me, 'Why are you laughing without any reason?' I wouldn't tell her why."

Bappa grew serious all of a sudden. "Better hurry up now," he said in a cold voice, "your parents must be waiting for your return. You are likely to get a sound whipping if you delay any longer."

Jhumjhum smiled at his words. "No hope," she said, "no one is bothered about what I do. If only they'd been strict with me I'd have thought that they were doing it for my own good. Because they care." She grew pensive for a few moments and suddenly asked him, "Could you come to our place every day? Then we'd be able to play table tennis together. Do you know how to play it?"

Bappa did not answer. He had longed to play table tennis ever since he joined college. He always made a beeline for the common room whenever he had a free period and watched the others play. But he was not brave enough to pick up the racquet and try since he did not know the game. Moreover, the table was perpetually monopolised by the senior students.

Jhumjhum could read his silence. "There's nothing to it, really," she said, "I'll teach you how to play. It was I who taught Baba to play, you know. I also taught Bipin, our cook." Her words brought on a feeling of constraint in Bappa's heart. He looked at her, realising that Jhumjhum's cordial words were meant to bring them closer. But somehow they merely increased the distance between them. For a moment he felt as though Jhumjhum was the image of a goddess who should be seen and admired from a distance and not be touched or manhandled.

Bappa had heard Jhumjhum's mother describe the house where they stayed so he could recognise it easily. But the sight that greeted him as he entered the garden stunned him. The garden was full of rocks and stones of different kinds and formations instead of plants. There were flowers in pots that were painted pink, blue and white. All around them were stones of many colours, beautifully arranged. At first he had thought that the stones were painted too. Then he realised that they were various mineral ores, brought up from the mines and cleaned up. They had streaks of white, golden or green.

"It's all Baba's doing," said Jhumjhum, laughing, "this is a geologist's garden, you see."

Bappa hesitated once more after crossing the threshold. There was a red carpet on the floor, thick and soft. Bappa wondered if he should walk on it with his shoes on or take them off. He remembered visiting the house of one of his college professors who was a Britisher, along with some other students. He had laughed at them when they took off their shoes. "My dear young friends, your shoes have had to put up with a lot of knocks on the streets," he had told them, "I've put the carpet on the floor in order to give them a little well-deserved comfort". Bappa had felt really embarrassed at his words at the time and remembered that people walked on carpets in the cinema theatres too. He took a few steps with his shoes on but stepped back once again to take them off. He did not feel like trampling on such a beautiful carpet in his dirty footwear.

"Maa, just come and see who is here," shouted Jhumjhum, "Actually, I forced him to come."

Bappa saw Jhumjhum's mother moving the heavy curtain on the door as she came into the room. The drawing room was so huge that it gave Bappa a feeling of discomfort and being alone.

"Dear me, aren't we lucky?" said Jhumjhum's mother as she came in. "Hello Bappa. Welcome to our place."

It was a beautiful room, artistically arranged with sofa sets, Japanese flower vases and other delightful accessories. Bappa walked up to a sofa and sat huddled up in a corner. He looked around and suddenly discovered that Jhumjhum was nowhere to be seen.

"Did Jhumjhum go to your place? Was she able to find it?" asked Jhumjhum's mother.

Bappa nodded bashfully and said, "Yes, she did. It was she who insisted on my coming here. My mother asked me to tell you that we can't make it to dinner this evening as my father isn't feeling too well..."

"What's wrong with him?" asked Jhumjhum's mother, interrupting him, "Not feeling well, you said? But he seemed fine this morning."

She sounded really anxious. Bappa liked her concern. It made her seem closely related. He had liked Jhumjhum's mother immensely when she had been to their place that morning. He liked her even more right now. She seemed like family and not just a fresh acquaintance.

Just then Jhumjhum came into the room. She had changed into a simple sari and had wrapped a shawl around her. She told her mother, "You'd better hear all about it from Bappa himself. I don't know anything about it." Then she jumped and sat on the sofa, bouncing twice as she did so. Bappa gave her a sidelong glance and asked, "Aunty, can you tell me why she has been addressing me as 'Bappa' all this time?"

"Quite right," said Jhumjhum's mother, "you should call him 'dada'."

"Dada, my foot!" cried Jhumjhum, making a face, "I wouldn't dream of addressing a kid like him as my elder!"

Jhumjhum's mother burst out laughing. "You'll never learn any manners!" she remarked.

Chapter 4

ANJALI heard Jhumjhum and Bappa playing table tennis in the adjacent room. The sound of their tapping racquets and laughter floated in as Jhumjhum scolded Bappa for his inability to play properly and teased him. Anjali could hear every word quite clearly despite being in a different room.

Anjali longed to chat with Bappa herself. There were so many things that she wanted to know about Anupam and his family in order to fill up the huge gap of twenty years. All these years she had been able to gather no more than stray scraps of information about Anupam. As for seeing him, she had been able to catch just two fleeting glimpses of him in the crowded city of Calcutta during the last twenty years—once, at a wedding reception, and another time, at a puja pandal. But the sight of Anupam had not turned her as restless as she felt now. She was at a loss to understand what had happened to her all of a sudden! Or why she felt it so acutely this time in Musabani. It is in this huge house that she suddenly discovered that she felt lonely—completely alone.

The house belonged to her husband's company. Everything, including the furniture, came along with it. The place was amply and beautifully furnished by the company so that people coming here on official work would not have to bother about furnishing it. With everything in its proper place, Anjali had to carry nothing from home. Jhumjhum had dragged the big dining table to the next room and got her father to set it up for table tennis. He had sent for the paraphernalia from Jamshedpur, the nearest big town. So, spending time had never been a problem for either of them.

Bipin, the domestic help, was dusting the furniture silently. He had switched on the lights a little while ago. Anjali, sitting in a corner of the big sofa, felt incredibly lonely in the huge and empty room. It was just the same in Calcutta. It was no use asking Jhumjhum to keep her company. She had her school friends and friends from the neighbourhood to keep her busy. And apart from friends, she had her games, activities, studies, music school and other involvements. But Anjali had nothing but memories. She visited relatives occasionally. Or else dropped in to see a movie. But it all seemed monotonous and meaningless!

Anjali's husband was busy writing his official report in his study. He would have to send it to the head office the next morning. Once his work was completed, he would come to this room and sit down. He would chat with her casually while they had their tea. But he would talk shop even then. There would be nothing interesting in his words. And yet, Anjali asked herself, wasn't she perfectly happy, technically speaking? Hadn't she managed to achieve everything that women like her dreamt of acquiring? She had enough money, a peaceful life and a devoted husband. What more could any woman ask for? But was she content? If not, what was the reason for her discontent? But despite thinking deeply she could find nothing to complain about! Perhaps an occasional quarrel with her husband would have added a dash of spice to her life!

Anjali grew absent-minded as she delved deeper into her thoughts. Was she thinking too much? Her husband had remarked a little while ago that she seemed to be turning into a philosopher, adding, "You'd better be careful, my dear! Geology just doesn't go with philosophy!" Anjali had laughed at his remark but had grown pensive once again.

As a matter of fact, her heart was longing to get back to Simla Street, to the time when she had been seventeen. It was a habit with her to re-live the past whenever she was alone. What was the harm? Hadn't twenty years of her life passed by doing just that, without any trouble or tension? But something strange had happened to her after seeing Anupam so unexpectedly at the weekly market the other day. A veritable storm had been raging within her heart ever since.

She might not have reacted like this had Anupam not looked away after their eyes met. She had discovered something in his expression in that single moment. Was it shame, anguish or just a shadow of insult? Or a sense of defeat? Anjali felt surprised to think that a grown up man should still carry the hurt caused by a tiny mistake so long ago or consider himself a defeated man because of it. Did he know about the thoughts and feelings she had been carrying in her heart for the last twenty years? The possibility that Anupam might never know about it brought tears to her eyes. Perhaps that's what prompted her to tell her husband excitedly, "You know, I met someone I knew ages back in the market this afternoon." Then she had added, "But I don't think he recognised me." Anjali had told him about the incident and Ranen had burst out laughing, saying, "You remind me of a poem I had read in my childhood about a parrot. It had settled down in a foreign land but when it saw a familiar face there it was so thrilled that it kept on fluttering its wings in excitement until it dropped down dead."

Anjali could not join in the laughter. Instead she said, "I am going to find out where he is staying. After all, this is a small place. Someone is bound to know where he is putting up if I mention his name."

"As her majesty wills!" said Ranen. Anjali laughed this time. But she felt that perhaps it would have been better for everyone concerned if she had not come across Anupam. The words they had exchanged were few but they brought on a tide of memories within her heart. She had never imagined that it could be like this. She felt even lonelier than before although waves of delight rose within her heart, one after the other, rising and falling rhythmically. She got lost in her thoughts once again.

Anupam da, you say that you remember me but can you tell me when I discovered you first?

Anjali was seated on the sofa with her eyes closed as she recalled scenes from the past. She had always sat very close to Anupam in her dreams and spoken to him as much as she chose. In fact, she had admitted as much to Anupam that evening when she told him, "I have been speaking to you within my heart for the last twenty years!" and that is exactly what she wanted to do right now. But the sound of the young players in the next room—Jhumjhum's loud laughter and the argument and teasing that followed—interrupted her dreams every time.

Anjali held a colourful English film magazine in her hand but did not feel like turning the pages. As she closed her eyes she saw her seventeen-year-old self. The narrow lane where they lived, a few steps away from Cornwallis Street, the sound of passing tram cars and buses, the Punjabi bus driver collecting fares in his tin box, the impatient honking of passing cars, the constant tapping sound in the shops of the goldsmiths and the general din of a mixed crowd. But the moment one entered Simla Street it was quiet and peaceful. If one walked further along the street one came across the big cowshed and a group of Bihari milkmen singing *Ramdhun* in a chorus. There was a sweet shop right next door where a roaring fire burnt all day and there were huge piles of ashes in the morning.

During winter, little beggar boys slept on the ashes in the dead of night for the sake of a little warmth.

Anjali could see it all in a series of moving pictures. There was the three-storeyed house they lived in. It was their ancestral home, each brother owning a different storey. But they shared a common kitchen, although everything else was separate. The cousins spent their spare time chatting on the terrace, whispering secrets or flying kites. Ah, how sweet were those days! Anjali lived in the third storey. Anupam stayed in the house across the road. The room right opposite Anjali's own belonged to Anupam and Bilu, his younger brother. Bilu must have been around eleven or twelve at the time, the same age as herself. Anjali had not been aware of Anupam's existence then.

"You say you remember everything but can you tell me when I first discovered you?"

"How should I know when you discovered me? I can only speak for myself. I discovered you when Runu, your cousin who lived on the ground floor..."

"Dear me, do you mean to say you still remember Runu's name? I am feeling jealous, you know. Why? Obviously because Runu was very pretty! That is why you haven't forgotten her."

"Really, Anjali, you are quite crazy! Is that your idea of beauty? I haven't forgotten her because she is mixed up with my memories of you. Don't you remember how, one day, you both stood whispering below the stairs when nobody was around? There was a long balcony just in front of my room where I was standing. I had looked at you once or twice when Runu whispered something in your ears and you looked up shyly."

"Yes...yes, that's just how it was! So you do remember everything? Even after all these years? But I had noticed you long before that. You would read late into the night, bending over your books and I would keep awake..."

Suddenly someone switched off the light. Anjali, interrupted in her reverie, cried out, "Who is it?"

Ranen laughed and switched on the light once again. He was holding his pipe in his left hand and poking it with a matchstick. He said, "I had switched off the light because I thought you were trying to snatch a siesta."

Anjali felt embarrassed. Where would all this day-dreaming lead to? Was she going insane? She hadn't realised when she had closed her eyes while thinking of Anupam. What could she do? One couldn't dream with one's eyes open!

Bipin came into the room and left their tea on the table.

"So they couldn't make it today? I understand Anupam babu is not feeling too well," said Ranen.

"Yes," replied Anjali. "But who told you?"

"Jhumjhum. I thought she would call me to play with her but she told me, 'I don't require you today. I've captured your goody-goody good boy instead!'"

Anjali laughed. But grew absent-minded immediately.

Ranen called out to Bipin, who came in and stood before him, duster on his shoulder.

"What are you cooking tonight?" Ranen asked him. "Chicken or egg curry? I wish I could have *khichuri* tonight."

"Then why didn't you tell me?" asked Anjali. "Or don't you like my cooking any more?"

Anjali stood up and told Bipin, "I'm coming to the kitchen."

Ranen grabbed her by the hand and pulled her down. "Sit down, will you? You can go to the kitchen later." Bipin left the room soon after. Ranen looked at the door and said, "I feel a sudden urge to sweet talk with you right now."

"Don't be absurd!" said Anjali with a serious face. Ranen burst out laughing. "In that case, let's go and watch the children playing."

As he stood up, Anjali stood up too and said, "Better drop your idea of having *khichuri* tonight. Tomorrow is the weekly market day. I'll get fresh green peas from there for your *khichuri*."

Anjali had reminded herself several times in the course of the day that tomorrow was the day for the weekly market. Normally it was Bipin who got the vegetables and other things from there. Her going the other evening had been a mere accident. But now the market pulled her like an addiction. That is why she mentioned it to her husband, although there was no need. She knew very well that it would never occur to him to question her sudden desire for visiting the market or doubt her in any way. He just wasn't the kind to mind such things. But Anjali could not help feeling a twinge of conscience because her sole reason for going there was because she wanted to meet Anupam. It made her feel somewhat lighter to admit that she was going to the market.

As they entered the next room, they saw Bappa putting up quite a good show.

Jhumjhum cried out, "Just see what a good teacher I am! Don't you think Bappa is playing quite well given that he has been at it for such a short time?"

"You kept him confined to this room the whole time!" said Anjali, laughing. Her laughter held a touch of complaint as she said, "I wanted to have a chat with him too."

Bappa stopped playing and threw down the racquet on the table, a shy expression on his face, as he said, "I'd better call it a day. It's quite late already."

Chapter 5

ANUPAM had come to the market quite early. Having completed his shopping, he turned to Budhli and said, "You can go home now, Budhli. I shall return after some time."

There was a lively cock-fight going on at one corner of the market, which was getting crowded rapidly. It was 'the' big attraction at the weekly market and people turned up from distant villages to enjoy the show. Some people brought along their own fighter cocks to participate in the betting—either for money or for gaining the cock itself. They were surrounded by an eager mob of Santhal men and women enjoying the fight, dancing joyfully when their chosen cock won and moaning loudly if it lost the round.

Anupam's eyes searched the entire market place eagerly. No, Anjali had not come. He had consulted his watch and had turned up exactly at the same time, hoping she would be here. He did not feel like returning home. After all, there was no harm in waiting a little. As he approached the cock-fighting area, two of the Santhal girls looked at him and smiled. Then they moved a little to make way for him. One of the men said, "Move over and let him watch the fight."

Two hefty men sat face to face, each with a sturdy cock, as they discussed the betting amount. Anupam saw them tying a sharp knife to the leg of the cocks. Immediately the crowd split into two parts. It was not as if the people knew the fighters or their owners personally, but somehow whenever a cock-fight took place the watching crowd invariably divided into two, each supporting a different side. No matter which side won, there was always a group to rejoice in the victory while the other side looked glum. Perhaps such is human nature, always bent on taking sides in any kind of rivalry.

As Anupam stood watching, the owners of the two cocks set them loose and they jumped at one another like two convicted murderers, bent on butchering each other. Blood gashed out as the knife of one cock struck the other, turning the white feathers a lurid crimson, followed by a cry of jubilation from the watching crowd. The loser pulled out the knife from the leg of the defeated cock and the winner grabbed it eagerly. Anupam could not stand the sight of blood so he walked away from there.

Two Santhal lads looked at him curiously, their eyes wide open.

One of them said, "Just look at his kurta. Isn't it too long!"

"Town folk always wear long kurtas," replied the other with the air of a know-all.

Anupam burst out laughing when he realised that it was the length of his kurta that they were talking about. He was about to make a retort when his eyes fell on the road and he saw Anjali walking down the uneven path, a pretty Manipuri embroidered bag in her hand. His heart missed a beat at the sight. He walked forward towards her, gazing at her with adoring eyes, his heart fluttering wildly. Anjali saw him from a distance, smiled and looked down. Her whole body swayed like a storm-driven branch while she walked, but when she saw Anupam she regulated her steps to a gentle pace.

"I'd have felt terrible if you hadn't come here today," she told him with a smile. Instantly Anupam's heart was reduced to petals of bliss. He merely smiled at her but said nothing.

"You must be very angry with me, for turning up at your place so suddenly that afternoon. Aren't you?"

"I've never had the strength of mind to be angry with you, Anjali. Neither before nor now," said Anupam in a quiet voice. "You have no idea what your visit meant to me."

Anjali lifted her eyes and looked at him curiously.

"Your visit gave me back the heart of a nineteen-year-old boy," said Anupam.

Anjali smiled bashfully. "How well you know the art of stringing words! You know, I was really afraid of offending you."

Anupam did not reply. He merely stepped along beside Anjali, feeling strangely exhilarated. She was so close, he could have easily touched her and held her hand. But he preferred the distance between them.

Anjali suddenly stopped walking and said, "Wait. We shall talk for a long time today. That is why I have asked Bipin to come later and pick up whatever else is needed for cooking. I shall merely pick up some fresh peas and a few other things for my husband." Anjali looked into his eyes and smiled. "He wants to have *khichuri* for dinner. After all, he was the one who had located your guest house. Don't you think he deserves a prize?"

Anupam smiled and said, "I can see that you are really happy, Anjali, and the knowledge makes me very happy too." Anjali stood silently for a while. Then she said, "Really happy? Perhaps I am! I can't find anything to feel sorry about. And yet the anguish I've often felt..." Her words were drenched in tears as she continued, "It's something you have never understood...something you will never understand..."Anjali tried to laugh. "Wait. I must buy the green peas for my husband."

An old Santhal woman sat under a tree, selling green peas. Anjali bent over the basket as she selected them. Anupam realised that Anjali was feeling embarrassed for being so frank. He turned the other way and saw a Punjabi gentleman and his stout wife buying tomatoes a little further down. There were also a few Bengali and Bihari shoppers as well and some totally unknown faces. Anjali stuffed the peas in her bag, paid for them and stood up.

"Give me the bag," said Anupam.

"Are you crazy? You are a professor, after all. How could I possibly let you carry a mere shopping bag?" said Anjali, laughing.

He said, "I don't like your addressing me so formally, Anjali."

Anjali stopped abruptly at his words and looked into his eyes.

Anupam tried to say something but Anjali was already arguing about the price of a cauliflower. The young Santhal girl selling it shook her head, laughing. "Pay me ten more paise, queen mother—" their usual mode of addressing a young and obviously rich customer."

Anjali shook her head. "No, not a paisa more."

"I'm asking for just ten paise," pleaded the girl, looking at Anupam. "Why don't you tell her, good sir?"

Anjali started and looked at Anupam, smiling shyly. Then she paid the girl another ten paise.

As they walked towards the stall where tomatoes were piled up, Anjali asked in a low voice, "I hope your wife did not suspect anything that afternoon. I was really nervous."

Anupam laughed loudly. "What could she suspect?"

"About our relationship?"

"But there was no relationship!"

"Wasn't there?" Anjali looked surprised. "Are you suggesting that there was nothing between us?"

Anupam looked into Anjali's eyes that were full of unshed tears. He felt a tremor all over his body. His voice grew tense with feeling as he asked, "In that case, why didn't you let me know about it, Anjali? Why couldn't you tell me right then?"

He paused for a while and said, "If only I had guessed how you felt…even this much! I myself had built so many castles in the air, Anjali…"

Anjali remained silent for a long time without replying to his question. Then she said, "But you were so much older than me, knew so much more than I did about everything. Why didn't you try to find out yourself? Why couldn't you understand the fear, nervousness or shyness of a seventeen-year-old girl?"

No one spoke for a while. Then Anjali said, "That's all. I don't need to buy anything more. Come, let's go back."

Anjali's last words, "Come, let's go back," echoed and re-echoed in Anupam's heart. He sighed. Yes, there was nothing more to do except turn back. As they walked back on the uneven road, Anjali suddenly said, "I had sent you a bouquet of roses when you were awarded your PhD. But I had not put my name on the card."

Anupam looked at Anjali, bewildered. "You? *You* sent it?"

Anjali looked at him, surprised. Her face grew ashen as she said in a broken voice, "What! Do you mean to tell me that you never guessed? Don't you ever understand anything?"

Anupam read the disappointment in Anjali's face and did not know what to say. But he could suddenly feel the soft touch of that bouquet in his hands and the rose petals brushing against his cheeks. How could he have imagined that the bouquet was from someone he had never spoken to and who had merely insulted him? Had he known that it was a gift from her, his joy would have been far greater than his delight in having achieved a doctorate.

"Strange!" said Anupam in a quiet voice. "I remember the incident so clearly. I was just twenty-four then. There was no name on the card. The florist's man had left the bouquet with my brother Bilu because I wasn't home at the time. He had left no name or address either."

"But there was a message on the card," said Anjali, walking in the opposite direction.

"I remember," said Anupam. "It said, 'From one who is the happiest person today'. My eldest sister teased me about it but I was clueless about the sender's identity. My younger sister told Anita about it after we were married and she had laughed heartily."

"Is that so?" asked Anjali as she burst out laughing. Then she said, "Just look at that girl! Isn't she crazy?"

Anupam looked towards the open field where the land was as uneven as waves, giving the place the look of an ocean belonging to prehistoric times.

Anupam recognised Jhumjhum and Bappa running down the slope. Jhumjhum was wearing a violet sari, the wild wind playing with her *anchal* and loose hair. She looked like a beautiful painting that was a part of Nature.

Anjali said, "Bappa has already become a close friend of Jhumjhum."

"They are lucky to have something that was never within our reach," said Anupam.

Chapter 6

It was fast becoming an addiction with Anupam. He longed to have Anjali near him all the time and to hear her speak without break. He had been hoping to meet her right from the morning and looked at his watch every now and then because he was afraid of arriving too late. What if Anjali should leave the market if he made her wait too long? And yet there was a time when he hated visiting the weekly market and found it tiring. It was Anita who would insist on his going.

Anupam thought of Anjali as he switched on the radio. The place was silent enough and seemed positively lonely without the sound of the wireless. The ropeway carrying buckets of copper was right over the guest house. The constant humming of their movement sounded like rain. But the ropeway was quiet now. Anjali had spoken just two words with him during their meeting last evening, thereby adding to his lonesomeness.

Anupam brought his shaving kit to the verandah overlooking the courtyard and started getting ready for his trip to the market. Anita came to spread the clothes for drying and said, "You know, we ought to visit them once this evening. They have asked us to go to their place so many times." Anupam was thrilled inwardly but did not show too much enthusiasm, saying casually, "Yes, we could drop in sometime this evening." But when it was evening he felt hesitant about reminding Anita. What if she saw through his put-on indifference? Had she by any chance realised the truth about them?

He wanted to tell her about it.

You know, Anita, I was once in love with a girl? But it was nothing like what you would imagine. We merely looked at each other. It was during our stay in Simla Street. How old was I? The same age as Bappa, I guess. I used to be scared by nature and also very foolish. I simply did not have the courage to take any kind of initiative. You never knew my father—he had a hair-trigger temper and was extremely reserved. And my mother was the sort who would frown if I dared to glance at a pretty face whenever we travelled by tram or bus. Between the two, I could never develop a personality of my own and just remained a goody-goody, obedient son.

But you know, there is something within the heart that refuses to listen to reason and fears nobody. We had a long verandah from one end to the other, right in front of the house, from where I could see a girl. She would stand in a corner of their terrace, holding on to the railing. She laughed and joked with her friends, seemingly unaware of my presence. Sometimes she would comb her hair while talking. I loved to look at her flowing tresses. I could also see her study table from there. She would pretend to be absorbed in her book and then suddenly lift up her eyes and look at me, happy in the awareness that I was looking at her too. That is how we had fallen in love. Eyes can say much more than mere words. Believe me, Anita, I had never actually spoken to her. And yet I knew her voice, her laughter and her footsteps. I had tried to speak to her just once. But she sent me back—insulted and humiliated. That was how we had parted. We left Simla Street soon after and moved elsewhere. I had quite believed that those days of youthful folly had been wiped off my life forever. But I realised after full twenty years that nothing ever gets lost. Yes, Anita, the girl I am speaking of is none other than Anjali.

Anupam wondered if Anita would understand if he actually spoke to her like this. No, there was no point in hurting her unnecessarily. He would keep this a secret from her. After all, every human being has a secret or two! It possible to share a good many things with one's wife, friend or sweetheart. But there are a few things that cannot be shared with anyone. Everyone has a coffer of private thoughts in his or her heart. But if you try to force it open, a truant bee may come out and sting you badly. Anjali was his pride. She deserved to remain hidden in his heart of hearts.

Just then Anita came into the room and said, "Should we go, then? If we do, I'll have to get ready." Anupam assented listlessly, trying to hide his eagerness.

He left the place with Anita and Hasu. As they went out they felt the gentle warmth of the evening sun. There were narrow trenches along the road, containing layers of kainite, with streaks of golden fibre gleaming in the sun. A cold breeze was blowing off and on. A little way past their guest house stood a building with a garden which the local people referred to as the "Nawab Bari". The house stood empty throughout the year with just a gardener in charge. Anupam had once thought of getting some flowers from the garden for the flower vases in their drawing room. But he no longer felt like it these days.

Anupam was carrying his jacket. "Why don't you wear it?" said Anita, "I don't want you to catch a cold."

"No, I'll wear it at the time of returning home," said Anupam. Ever since he met Anjali he felt conscious about his age. He continued to recall the incident of the afternoon and all that Anjali had said.

Anita gave Anupam a sidelong glance and said, "Bappa hasn't said anything more about returning to Calcutta." Her tone was significant.

Anupam felt annoyed and looked at Hasu. "It's not what you think," he said. "Their generation is different and they think differently."

"I didn't suggest anything," said Anita. "Bappa is quite different from other boys. I'd have guessed from his face if it had been anything like that."

Anupam felt uncomfortable. Did Anita suspect anything by looking at his face? Heaven alone knew! He felt slightly nervous. Would she guess anything after seeing Anjali's face that evening? Changing the subject, he said, "I suppose Bappa has reached their place already. He was telling me about his game of table tennis this morning."

They had reached the country liquor shop by now, where a big group of coolies working in the mine had already collected, squatting in a circle. Whiffs of country liquor floated in the air. Anita covered her nose and walked faster.

As the party reached the guest house, Ranen welcomed them excitedly. He seemed even more delighted because their visit was unexpected. Anjali also came out of the house smiling and grabbed Anita's hands. Then she laughed and said, "I've a serious complaint to make," Anita was charmed by the cordiality of her voice. She had liked Anjali when she visited them for the first time but she had not felt as close to her as she did now. They had both been much more formal then.

Anita laughed and said, "You have been complaining right from the start, haven't you?"

"From the start?" asked Anjali curiously.

"Wasn't it so? When you came for the first time, hadn't you come to complain about my husband not having recognised you at the weekly market?" Anita burst out laughing as she looked at Anupam and Ranen.

Ranen was tall, smart and handsome with a sharp, aquiline nose and looked good in his white woollen trousers and a knitted wool pullover. The pattern in white and navy blue was perhaps a bit childish for his age but it suited him wonderfully, making him look almost ten years younger. He pointed at Anjali with his finger and said, "Serves you right!"

Everyone burst out laughing. Anjali wanted to ask Anita why they had cancelled the invitation just because Anupam had caught a slight cold. Anita understood and replied, "We didn't come that evening because we'd have had a problem if we returned late that night. His cold would get worse and he wouldn't have let any of us sleep with his non-stop sneezing!" Once again everyone laughed loudly followed by a sudden abrupt silence, as though no one had anything more to say.

Anjali promptly said, "Please come inside."

One by one, everyone walked in and saw that Bappa and Jhumjhum were just about to leave. Anita saw them and said, "Where are you off to, Jhumjhum? I came here all this way to chat with you and..."

"Please, Aunty, don't stop me now. The sun is about to set and soon there won't be any light left."

Jhumjhum looked at Anita and her parents with tragic eyes.

"Oh, very well. But do return soon," said Anita, smiling. She also gave her a careful look. Jhumjhum was wearing an off-white sari with moss-green stripes and a brown border. She looked slim, trim and beautiful. A big camera hung from her shoulder and Anita guessed that they were going to photograph either the Shurgi Hill or its beautiful surroundings.

"Please don't lose my camera," Ranen shouted after them. Everyone laughed.

"She has her own camera but always insists on taking mine," said Ranen, "She has been after me since this morning."

"You pamper her far too much," said Anjali, trying to sound angry.

"It's only natural," said Anita, "who wouldn't pamper such a lovely girl? How well the sari suits her! Your daughter is a real beauty, you know."

"I think Hasu has a much sweeter face," said Anjali and looked at her. "Come, Hasu. Come and sit near me." Hasu shook her head shyly and did not move from her place.

Anjali looked at Anita. "As for the sari, it is mine but it quite suits her. Jhumjhum insisted on wearing it and I'm quite sure she'll manage to tear it before she comes home."

All this talk was lost on Anupam. He was busy looking around him. The thick carpet and the heavy, bulky sofa set in the drawing room made him feel quite distant from the others. In fact, he had been feeling slightly uncomfortable at first. But despite sitting so far apart, whenever he glanced at Anjali, he was able to take in every detail of her body—the way she sat, her smile and everything else about her. After all, how much could proximity contribute to one's ability to see and feel things?

Suddenly there was a lull when everyone stopped talking. The total silence seemed to imply that there was nothing more to be said. Anupam looked at Anjali. It seemed to him that she had turned into an idol of a benign deity with a gentle smile, drowned in a sea of memories. Anupam remembered that during those days of youth whenever he looked at her with mute pain and tears in his heart, his glance was transformed to that of a worshipper looking at a deity when offering flowers in worship. Anjali really looked like a deity now.

"Do you know, you still walk just the way you used to, with your head bent and your eyes fixed on the ground," said Anjali, smiling at Anupam.

Ranen stretched his legs and leaned on the sofa as he remarked, "Those who hold a high place in society, normally bend their heads while walking."

This time it was Anita who laughed. "Really? Did he also walk like that when he was young? I thought he had got into the habit later because of having to bend over the answer-papers of his students all the time."

Ranen laughed out loudly at Anita's remark. But Anupam could not bring himself to laugh. In fact, he hadn't even heard Anita. He was still thinking of Anjali's words as he silently spoke to himself: *Anjali, during those days you too walked the same way, with your head bent low. You attended the morning session at Vidyasagar College. I was not used to waking up so early in the morning as a rule.Nevertheless I would wake up at the crack of dawn and stand in a corner of the verandah in order to catch a glimpse of you. I could not see you in your room so I stood with my gaze fixed on the door downstairs. After a while as I heard the sound of the door opening, I could feel the rush in my veins. You looked up at my verandah for a moment when our eyes met. Your glance seemed to place a rosebud in the buttonhole of my shirt. The name of that rosebud was 'bliss'. Then you would walk away with quiet steps. I hoped against hope that you would look up again. But you wouldn't. And yet, that single glance of yours kept me sated for the whole day. I would leave for my college before you returned from yours. I held you within my imagination until the evening. Once in a while we would come face to face with each other but you would look down as soon as our eyes met. But it made me feel as though I had you beside me as I paced the whole world.*

"Bipin!" Anjali called Bipin and went inside with him. Anupam shook himself awake from his dreams and looked at her before she left. He did not feel like sitting down quietly because he felt restless. Ranen was a perfect gentleman and Anita seemed to get on with him quite well. But Anupam felt annoyed with both of them at the moment. All he wanted was to speak to Anjali in quiet seclusion. That is why the presence of other people—no matter who they were—seemed intolerable.

Anita stood up when she saw Anjali leaving the room. Anupam could guess what she would do next. She would tell Anjali, "Won't you show me your house?" Anupam could visualise Anita going to each room and looking carefully at everything as she tried to calculate the cost of each item and thereby find out how rich they were. She would ask how many servants she had and what she usually cooked and compare Anjali's situation with her own. Perhaps the difference would hurt her and she would comment about it after reaching home. Or else criticise her. But Anita merely told Anjali, "What a lovely house you have. The rooms are so spacious!"

"Too spacious!" said Anjali, putting down the dishes of snacks. "It's just the three of us. It feels positively scary if I suddenly wake up at night."

Anupam picked up a *kachuri* made of green peas and said, "This is absolutely delicious and also my most favourite snack." His eyes met Anjali's as he looked up from his plate and there was a silent exchange of words. Anjali smiled and said, "I've tasted so many kinds of snacks but I still remember eating *phuchka* from a roadside stall during the pujas long ago, the taste of which I've never forgotten."

Ranen did not understand the implication of her words. He smiled and said, "Everything tastes different when one is young!"

Yes, everything about youth was different! Anupam thought, how strange that Anjali should still remember that he used to be fond of green-peas *kachuri* once upon a time. Stranger still that she should remember that once when Bilu and Anjali had gone out to the puja pandal together and came across Anupam accidentally, Bilu had asked him for some money and the two of them had eaten *phuchkas* together. Anjali held the rough bowl made of sal leaves carefully as she ate the *phuchkas* but had not spoken a single word with him. Anupam could suddenly see the entire scene clearly as he remembered every detail. If Anjali had not forgotten the taste of childhood, neither had he!

Chapter 7

JUHUMJHUM marched out of the room, the camera swinging on her shoulder, followed by Bappa. As their eyes met, Jhumjhum gave him a matey grin.

"That was a narrow escape!" she said, "We'd have got stuck at home otherwise."

She paused for a while before adding, "Of course aunty is an absolute poppet. But, tell me, do you enjoy talking to old people?"

Bappa tried to look serious as he replied, "They're not really old."

"Of course they are!" said Jhumjhum. "Baba has quite a few grey hairs already."

Jhumjhum looked around and tugged at the sleeve of Bappa's shirt. "Run or else the light will fade completely. Hurry up!"

There was a mound a little further away, made of loose soil dug up from the mines long ago. It looked like a small hillock beyond which lay green fields, rows of trees and a little Santhal village. One of the cottages had a saffron- and- slate-coloured border on the walls, where someone had made a drawing of a tiger dragging a man in its mouth. The man, despite hanging precariously, had struck an arrow at the neck of the tiger. Bappa and Jhumjhum had already seen the drawing before but did not have a camera with them at that time.

Jhumjhum tugged Bappa's shirt once again. "Come on, run!" She started running too. Running side by side, they got breathless and burst out laughing as they huffed and puffed.

Jhumjhum was looking very pretty in her mother's sari. Bappa laughed when he saw her trying to manage it and keep the folds in place while the camera swung wildly from her shoulder as she ran. Running beside her, Bappa enjoyed the scene, especially Jhumjhum's running figure. They stopped running after a while and changed into a steady trot as they approached the cottage. Bappa noticed that Jhumjhum was sweating, although it was winter. Drops of sweat stood on her face and gleamed brightly in the rays of the setting sun. Why bother to snap the Santhal village, he thought. It would be far better to take a snap of Jhumjhum instead and take it right now. Then he'd be able to look at it whenever he wanted.

But Jhumjhum had no time to think along those lines. She walked up to the cottage. An old woman sat in the sun with a piece of sacking wrapped around her while a naked boy ate something from a mud bowl. Jhumjhum adjusted the lens of her camera, focused it and snapped. Then she took another and yet another, taking photos wherever she looked. Then she laughed and said, "It's great fun taking photographs on Baba's camera as one can take thirty-five of them at one go. Mine gets exhausted the moment I start snapping."

Bappa wanted to take a photograph of Jhumjhum in these surroundings and suddenly said, "Give me the camera for a moment. I want to take one of you."

"Me?" asked Jhumjhum, looking surprised. Then she laughed loudly. "What on earth for?"

Bappa's face grew glum at her words as he tried to fathom what she meant.

"Oh! I say, don't move," cried Jhumjhum, taking a snap of Bappa. He turned his face and she took another. She burst out laughing as she kept on snapping him, one after the other. Bappa looked annoyed. "You could have told me frankly that you don't want me to touch your camera!" he said.

"Wait," cried Jhumjhum, "please, let me take another. You look so nice when you puff up your cheeks in anger." She took another photo of him and then handed him the camera. "Here you are! No need to get so mad. Take as many pictures of me as you want to."

Bappa smiled, took the camera from her hand and adjusted the aperture.

"You'd better tell me how you want me to pose," said Jhumjhum. Bappa took several shots of her. In one, he made her stand near the drawing of the tiger.

Jhumjhum laughed. "So you paired me off with the tiger finally?"

"You are in a tiger's grip already," replied Bappa in a serious voice.

Jhumjhum pretended not to hear him. Then she suddenly said, "Come on, Bappa, walk fast. It's going to be dark very soon. Aunty and Uncle must be waiting for you."

Bappa repeated what Jhumjhum had told him a little while ago, "I don't like chatting with old people."

They were walking along the uneven path towards the guest house. But Jhumjhum did not laugh at his words and continued to walk silently. Gradually the path grew steep and Jhumjhum leaned on Bappa's shoulder as she walked. Then she said in a serious voice, "You know, Bappa, sometimes I feel really sorry for Baba." Bappa held her hand as they climbed up the raised mound and climbed down again and asked, "Why?"

"I don't know," said Jhumjhum in a pained voice. "I've been noticing for a few days that Baba is often lost in his thoughts and notices nothing around him. I also know that he didn't sleep a wink last night."

Bappa looked at Jhumjhum in surprise. "Didn't sleep a wink?"

"No, he didn't," said Jhumjhum. "When I woke up at night, I saw Baba standing in front of the window, staring at the darkness outside. I felt positively scared to see him. When I woke up the next time, I saw Maa sleeping peacefully but Baba was seated on the easy chair. Could you tell me what the reason might be?"

Bappa looked down as he walked and replied, "I can't guess."

Jhumjhum sighed. She tried to say something but couldn't bring herself to say it as she felt embarrassed. She had been thinking deeply about her father's anxiety but could find no reason. For a moment, a sudden suspicion had crossed her mind. Was he worried about her? Was it because he did not like his friendship with Bappa and her roaming around with him? Or was it something else? Suddenly she burst out laughing. Bappa looked surprised. "What are you laughing for?" he asked.

"Nothing," said Jhumjhum, shaking her head. She walked in silence after that and did not speak for a long time.

"Jhumjhum," whispered Bappa in a deep voice.

"Yes?"

"May I ask you something?"

Jhumjhum nodded without looking at him.

"Jhumjhum, do you love anyone?" Bappa's voice held a strange mixture of tears and despair.

Jhumjhum burst out laughing. "No. I don't intend to get involved in anything like that. I don't trust boys of the present generation, throwing acid bulbs at the drop of a hat!" Then she paused for a while and said in a cool voice, "Perhaps acid bulbs are no longer in fashion! Are they, Bappa?"

Bappa did not reply.

There was so much he wanted to tell her, so much he had planned to say! But everything was topsy-turvy now. It was impossible to expect Jhumjhum to take anything seriously. She understood nothing, felt nothing! The tears in Bappa's eyes slipped into his heart and turned into a block of ice. They were close to Jhumjhum's house by now. The sun had set already. The blue sky was growing dark gradually. The air was heavy with the heady fragrance of wild flowers. Shadows of the tall trees took on the shape of giants. Just then a bird flew past, chirping merrily. There was a culvert ahead. A cold breeze was beginning to blow.

"I wish I had brought a cardigan," said Jhumjhum.

Bappa did not feel like talking but he said, "You'll reach home in a moment. What's the need for cardigans?"

"We are almost home," whispered Jhumjhum. "I wish we could sit here for a while. Should we?"

"Here?" asked Bappa, surprised, "Well, we could, I suppose."

They sat on the railing of the culvert. An old man passed by them, tapping his stick. They stared at him in surprise. The darkness grew deeper as they saw the lights coming from Jhumjhum's house. They sat in silence. Then Bappa whispered, "Jhumjhum!"

"Um?"

"When the film is printed will you give me a copy of the photos?"

"Of course, I will. Every single one of your photos. You were looking so angry! Some of them are bound to be priceless!"

Bappa did not reply at first. Then he said, "I don't want my photos."

Jhumjhum sounded surprised. "Which ones do you want then?"

"You must promise to give me one of yours."

Jhumjhum laughed and pretended to be surprised. "Mine? But what will you do with it?"

"I'll keep it with me," said Bappa. "We shall leave this place before long and we may never meet again. I shall see your photograph sometimes."

"But seeing a photograph is not the same as seeing a person! Really, Bappa, you are quite crazy! Photos are merely meant for showing other people, especially one's friends. If I ever feel like seeing you very badly, I am sure I shall go to your house."

"Will you really feel like seeing me, Jhumjhum?" asked Bappa eagerly, "Please tell me the truth."

Bappa's hand was resting on the culvert railing and it felt cold to touch. Jhumjhum laid her hand on his and said, "I don't know myself. I can never tell beforehand what I shall feel like."

Chapter 8

ANUPAM wanted to wash his hands after tea. The washroom was at the back of the house, at the end of a long corridor. He looked carefully at both sides as he walked, following close behind Anjali. She smiled at him curiously but did not speak. She felt happy that Anupam had come to visit her without being asked and the delight reflected on her face. She was not bothered about who listened to her words and who didn't, knowing that there was one person in the room who was drinking in every word she spoke. The rest simply did not matter. She spoke to her husband, Anita and Hasu on various subjects. Their days in Simla Street, Anupam's parents and his brother Bilu. She broke into laughter as she recalled some of the incidents. Anupam was aware that Anjali was happy and that all her words—no matter to whom they were addressed—were meant for him alone. He looked at her and found her eyes fixed steadily on him. He felt slightly embarrassed and glanced at Ranen and Anita to see if they had noticed it. He was afraid that Anjali was being a bit too daring and it made him apprehensive. He wanted to tell her, "There's no point in reviving memories, Anjali. Such boldness simply does not go with our present age." But he couldn't because it was something he had often wished to do himself.

After tea, Anupam had been wondering whether to wipe his hand with his handkerchief or dip it in the glass when Anjali asked, "Would you like to wash your hands? The wash basin is along the corridor." Anupam got up and followed Anjali. It was a very long corridor with a number of rooms on either side. But it was dark all around. As they walked on, Anjali looked at him, her eyes beaming with laughter. As they reached the end of the corridor, Anjali switched on another light. Anupam's heart was beating fast. For a moment he felt like switching off the light. Then he quickly glanced back at the drawing room. There were more rooms on the other side of the long corridor. He could see the light in one of them and also got a whiff of spices. Perhaps it was the kitchen and Bipin was cooking dinner. Or perhaps they had another cook. Anupam had no idea about Anjali's domestic staff. Anjali walked up to the wash basin and opened the tap for him. She stood close to him while he washed his hands. But no one spoke a word. Anupam was afraid of breaking the silence. Anjali smiled at him and said, "Do you feel afraid?"

Anupam did not reply. He was amazed to see Anjali behaving so normally. Wasn't she afraid that someone might hear them?

"I don't intend to be afraid any more," said Anjali.

"I didn't get you alone for a moment, Anjali," said Anupam, shedding his fear. Anjali laughed. She wet her hand and splashed a few drops of water on his face. She looked at Anupam in a way that made his heart quiver. It suddenly seemed as though they were no older than Bappa and Jhumjhum.

For the first time Anupam felt that he had entered a forbidden world. He had felt it the moment he stepped inside the corridor, a feeling of inebriation that made him forget that he was a married man with a family. The figures of Anita, Hasu and Bappa seemed to fade from his consciousness. It was like watching his family through a glass covered with raindrops where everything looked vague and indistinct. Even Ranen seemed like a piece of furniture whom one could shove anywhere at will.

When they had met at the market and walked back together, Anjali's voice had been full of unshed tears. But he had not felt that they were doing anything wrong. For the first time Anupam felt that this forbidden togetherness was strangely intoxicating. So was the secrecy they seemed to share. As he walked back to the drawing room with Anjali, his expression changed drastically. He looked at Ranen and said, "One can't make out what a large house this is from outside. Your corridor seemed to be endless!"

Ranen tried to smile at his words but it sounded like a sigh to Anupam. Anjali was already chatting with Anita. Hasu was still eating. After some time Anjali escorted Anita and Hasu to the corridor once again to take them to the wash basin. Anupam tried his best to get over his feeling of discomfort and looked at Ranen, who seemed to be lost in thoughts, his head bent. Anupam was beginning to feel embarrassed all over again. Did Ranen babu suspect anything? Could he have heard Anjali's words from here? And did Anita suspect something too? Anupam felt really uncomfortable at the possibility.

A strange silence pervaded the enormous room. Anupam and Ranen sat facing each other and yet neither of them looked at one another or uttered a single word. Was there a storm brewing? wondered Anupam uneasily. Or perhaps a lightning would strike the household after they'd have left the place. Anupam started sweating, although it was winter. Even if nothing happened right now, would Anjali have to face an unsavoury scene after they had gone home? Anupam felt really concerned about Anjali. He would never forgive himself if there was a misunderstanding between her and Ranen babu because of him. He was unable to lift his eyes or look at Ranen.

He could hear Anjali and Anita talking in the veranda and tried to make out what they were saying. But the sound was too low and muffled for comprehension. Anupam looked at the table in front of him and picked up the ashtray. He examined it carefully and fished out a packet of cigarettes from his pocket. He could feel the box of matches too but left it where it was. "May I have your lighter?" he asked Ranen, looking at him this time. Ranen looked up and handed him the lighter in silence. He seemed lost in his thoughts once again.

Anjali returned after seeing off Anupam and his family. With their departure, all of a sudden, the house seemed unbearably empty and unnaturally quiet. She heard Bipin working in the kitchen. But the sound seemed to enhance the silence rather than lessen it. Anjali felt that Anupam had gone home taking all her happiness with him. Anjali was surprised at herself. Anupam had been a mere memory for twenty years, someone she had remembered only occasionally. How could a few words with him bring on such havoc within her heart? Why did she long to be with him and crave to see him all the time, just the way she used to during those days of adolescence?

Jhumjhum, back a little while ago, was at the study table scribbling something. But Anjali felt no curiosity to find out what she was doing. Nor did she feel worried about her husband. Perhaps he was sitting somewhere smoking his pipe or else checking his office files. Anjali drew a chair and sat by the bedroom window, staring at the darkness outside. The night sky seemed solid black, broken by a few lights in the distance. The ropeway had stopped working by then, the continuous humming of the machine, gone.

"I can't! I just can't do it!" said Anjali to herself and sighed. She wanted to cry. Perhaps she would feel lighter if only she could cry and cry and cry for hours! That might cool the anguish she felt within her heart right now. Once again she was lost in her reverie.

I searched for you high and low when we were in Calcutta, looking for you everywhere I went. I looked at all the faces in the cinema hall, hoping to find yours in one of them. At Outram Ghat, at Maidan and at every exhibition I visited, I looked for you and wondered why I never met you anywhere. After all, you too must be visiting places! During the Durga puja I visited one puja pandal after another—sometimes with my sisters, sometimes with sisters-in-law and at times with my husband. Do you know why? Because I carried a tiny piece of hope in my heart that I'd come across you somewhere in the crowd. But my hope was never fulfilled. I never found you at any of these places and just returned home exhausted. And yet, it's not that I did not know where you lived. I knew your address. I came across Bilu on and off. I could keep abreast with all your news. I could have easily landed up at your place whenever I wanted, there was nothing to stop me, you see. Once when I had actually seen you at a wedding reception, I might have spoken to you if I so desired. But I had tightly held all my longings in leash. But now, now, you have suddenly severed all restraints and I can no longer hold myself.

Anjali suddenly felt totally helpless. Perhaps her husband did not really love her and never had! Perhaps love was something quite different. Something that she herself did not understand and never will. She tried to remember if her husband had ever waited for her eagerly but could not think of a single instance. It was she who had waited for him all her life and had felt impatient if he came home late. Perhaps her husband had also felt the same when she went out with others and got delayed. But that was mere anxiety. Neither of them had felt anything but anxiety, which was not the same as a lover's eager wait.

Anupam alone had waited for her. He stood at the verandah at the crack of dawn every day, knowing full well that he would get nothing in return. He stood there just for the sake of catching a glimpse of her. Something that lasted no more than a moment. Anjali had been to a wedding once and had returned home well after midnight, feeling tense and depressed because she was afraid Anupam had already gone to sleep. She had broken into tears when she looked up and saw Anupam still waiting for her. She knew that he could not sleep without seeing her before he turned in for the night. They had exchanged nothing but looks. She could never have imagined that a mere glance could leave such a deep impression within one's heart.

You read for a long time at night and then came and stood at the balcony, right opposite my room. And you would find that the light in my room was also on. We would look at each other steadily for a few moments. Then I would switch off the light and go to my bedroom. You would switch off yours and lie down beside Bilu, who was already asleep.

Anjali tried to remember if her husband had ever waited just for the sake of catching a glimpse of her. Had he noticed any change in Anjali? Did he suspect anything? Then she heard Jhumjhum switching off the light in her room. Perhaps she was already in bed. There was a door between her bedroom and theirs that she left open at night because Jhumjhum was afraid of sleeping all alone in this huge house. Anjali stared at the darkness outside the window for a while. Then she walked out of the room to the veranda. Bipin saw her and said, "Master is in the room at the end of the corridor." Anjali saw the light and walked towards the room. She paused at the door before going inside. Ranen seemed to be sleeping with his head on the table. Anjali went near him with quiet steps and touching his shoulder gently, she asked, "Were you sleeping?"

"What? No, I wasn't," said Ranen as he let out a sigh and sat up.

"Come to bed. What's the matter with you?" Anjali asked in an anxious voice.

"Nothing. Nothing at all." This time Anjali heard the sigh. She felt embarrassed. She had been noticing her husband's absent-mindedness for quite some time. Perhaps he was worried about something. There seemed to be a distance between them which she had never realised before. Was it because…?

Ranen stood up silently. Then he walked to the bedroom and got into bed. Anjali switched off the light, shut the door and lay down beside him. Although they were lying next to each other and both were awake, no one said a word.

Anjali wanted to reach out to her husband. What was he worrying about? About her? Then why didn't he say so frankly? She was ready to tell him everything and get it off her chest, holding back nothing!

"Do you want to tell me anything?" she whispered.

Ranen did not reply.

"What are you so upset about?" asked Anjali. "I have been watching it for some time now." Anjali felt like bursting into tears.

"Please go to sleep," said Ranen in a quiet voice. "I am not sleepy."

Anjali did not speak any more. She could hear her own heart beating. Would Ranen hear it too? After lying silently for a while, she said, "You didn't even speak to them properly this evening."

Once again Ranen did not reply.

Anjali lay in the darkness, staring at the dark ceiling. It seemed to her that a disc of light was revolving before her eyes, steadily, constantly. She turned and laid her hand on Ranen's arm and he laid his hand on hers. It seemed more like the touch of an unconscious man.

Chapter 9

ANITA hadn't given the matter much thought at first. She found it rather difficult to decide what was natural and what was not. Ever since getting married she had blindly depended on her husband's decisions in all matters. But these days she depended more on Bappa. There were many things she did not care to discuss with Anupam. She confided to Bappa instead and asked for his advice. She was really proud of her son.

Anita's father had been an employee of the post office. His job had been a transferable one. It had not been possible for Anita to go to college, but she had managed to clear her matriculation as a private student. Life had never been too easy for her. She had been accustomed to living on a shoe-string budget, getting used to denying herself many things and learning not to express her desire for things. She had continued to live the same way even after being married to Anupam. She had never felt the need to worry about him because she realised quite soon that his life totally revolved around teaching, attending college committees, checking test papers, giving tuitions and spending his holidays relaxing and chatting with his colleagues. Her friends were envious that a college professor had chosen her as his partner. Her father was also proud of the fact. Anita saw no reason to feel proud of her husband. But she was inordinately proud of Bappa. Whenever their relatives or friends dropped in for a visit, they invariably said, "You should be proud of your son. Boys like him are rare these days."

Anita believed it in her heart. A lot of boys were good at studies. But her dreams about Bappa were rather special. She didn't merely dream of his getting a good job and earning more money. It stretched far beyond such mundane considerations. Anita was not modern herself. Clinging to her old beliefs and values, she had never been able to keep pace with Anupam's ideas. She knew that it was just not possible for her to share the same wavelength as him. So she had merely learned not to contradict him. But Bappa was different. She wanted him to possess all those qualities that she held to be ideal. She wanted him to be modest, polite and honest. She discovered in him all the good qualities that she had read about in books. Someone had once remarked, "Bappa is too good for a practical life and quite unfit for the age we live in." The words had made Anita very angry. She wanted Bappa to remain just the way he was. He was a perfect match for a mother like Anita. He did not need to match anyone else.

Anita trusted Bappa implicitly, so she had not been afraid of his getting into any undesirable situation. Besides, Jhumjhum possessed a rare touch of innocence which she had found charming. She had seen nothing objectionable in their friendship. Although she had been a little apprehensive at first, Anupam had managed to laugh her out of it. But after returning from Anjali's place that evening, Anita could not help but feel a little worried.

"You know, Maa, you can't make out how large the house is from outside," Bappa had told her after his first visit to Anjali's place. Anita had seen the house herself and could not banish a feeling of discomfort since then. Was she jealous of Anjali's riches—the expensive carpet, the exclusive curtains and all that? Or was it some kind of inferiority complex because she couldn't get used to their ways?

"I had liked Ranen babu immensely when he came to our house for the first time," Anita had remarked on their way back home. "He seemed so jolly. But he seemed so preoccupied and unmindful this evening. Somehow I felt sorry for him."

Anupam had not said anything in reply. And Anita had not said what she really wanted to tell him. She had really liked Anjali, right from the first day. She was so cordial, so friendly and seemed to feel no pride for either her wealth or position. When Anjali had taken her for a wash along the long corridor, Anita had looked at the rooms on either side and remarked, "Your guest house is a regular palace compared to our tiny two-roomed one." Then she had burst out laughing. Anjali had not answered at first. Then she said, "You people can remain close to each other because your rooms are small. The larger a room, the greater the distance between its inhabitants." Then she had laughed and said on a different note, "Just look at my daughter! She doesn't seem to find this large house adequate and is always finding excuses to go out."

"Why don't you check her?" asked Anita. "It's your fault, not hers."

Anjali did not reply at first. Then said in a strange voice, "I just don't feel like checking her. I grew up amidst so many restrictions that I haven't the heart to impose them on anyone else."

Anjali's words now rang in Anita's ears. Anita too had grown up amidst restrictions galore. But she had never felt that it was something to protest against. If anything, she felt proud that she had been brought up so carefully and strictly. And because she had faced it herself, she had wanted to impose the same restrictions on her children too. She saw nothing strange or wrong about it. She had not forbidden Bappa to make friends with Jhumjhum and the prospect did not make her feel nervous. But when the two of them returned home so late that evening, something in Bappa's face had made her heart skip a beat for a moment. And she had looked at Jhumjhum's face repeatedly. Anita was afraid of darkness and still more afraid of their age. But neither Anjali nor Ranen had batted an eyelid, as though it was the most natural thing under the sun to return home so late.

And Jhumjhum had seemed the least conscious of all, making a regular racket the moment she stepped inside the room.

"Here's your camera, Baba, all safe and sound! Really, can't you trust even a simple gadget to me without feeling nervous?" said Jhumjhum. "I'm afraid Bappa and I have used up the entire reel. And I have taken one great shot—you can't imagine how fantastic!" She then turned to her mother and said, "You'd better check your sari," and she turned around like a model walking the ramp. "Have I torn or damaged it in any way? Aunty is here—she can vouch for it too. I can't think why you are so scared to let me wear your things!"

Then she had sat down next to Anita, huddling up against her and burst out laughing. "You know, Aunty, Maa is such a spoilsport. She doesn't wear the saris herself and won't let me wear any either!" Anjali had also laughed at her words.

"You keep quiet," she told her, "I've lost track of how many of my saris you have ruined!"

Jhumjhum didn't seem to hear her words and stood close to her father. "Please, Baba, do send the photos for printing to Jamshedpur tomorrow and ask them to be quick," she said pleadingly, "Won't you?" Ranen had nodded in agreement.

As she remembered the scene and Jhumjhum's endearing ways, Anita's feelings of vague discomfort vanished. Nevertheless, she wanted to protect Bappa the way one protected saplings. By keeping it in a cage of wire. Or else build a protective brick wall around him. She had seen many such protected saplings around the Maidan some years ago. They were full-fledged trees now, after the rains. Once her own tree grew old enough to provide shade to the others, she wouldn't be afraid any more.

Anita wanted to speak to Anupam about it the next morning so that he might think of a solution? Bappa had initially been so unwilling to stay here! Couldn't Anupam tell him, "Why don't you return to Calcutta since you don't like this place?" or couldn't Anupam think of some other excuse to send him away? But before she could say anything, Jhumjhum dropped in at their place and said, "Bappa, didn't you say you wanted some music? I've a whole pile of new records here. Please go and fetch your record-player." Anita felt relieved. After all, they would be merely listening to music right under her eyes! She showed her the record player and said, "I saw the beautiful radiogram at your place the other day."

Jhumjhum rolled her eyes and said, "Gracious, Aunty! You don't know the kind of restrictions I have to face at home! I wouldn't be allowed to play any Hindi songs on our radiogram because Baba would plug his ears and Maa would look as though she has swallowed a bitter pill!"

Anita could not help laughing at her words and Bappa said, "What a low taste you have! Even I don't like Hindi film music." Jhumjhum ignored his words and placed the record on the player. Then she sat on the bed comfortably and listened to one record after another, shaking her head and swaying her body in rhythm with the music. Anita felt like laughing and moved away. Bappa was seated at another end of the bed. He too was tapping his feet to the music unconsciously. Jhumjhum looked at him suddenly and said, "What a low taste you have—tapping your feet to the music of Hindi songs! Shame on you!"

Chapter 10

Anupam kept himself confined to his house for the next few days. He realised that the entire episode of what he had been going through for the last few days seemed ridiculous at his age. Something utterly ludicrous. He was sure that if his friends got to know about it they would also feel the same. But he had little control over himself. Whenever he was alone, he couldn't help longing for Anjali's presence and craving to meet her all alone. The mind does not age with the body! He wanted to call out to her and tell her, "Anjali, you have lost a great deal of time and delayed too much. Far too much!"

He had built up so many dreams that centred around her once upon a time. But it was no longer possible to fulfil them. Somehow the very intensity of that longing had vanished from his life. Otherwise, he too might have felt tempted to rush around her in the soft glow of the winter evening, like young Bappa. Perhaps he would have taken Anjali in his arms if he found a spot of wilderness. Life seemed to be full of colours whenever he delved into his memories, even now. But there was also a streak of pain that gnawed inside and refused to stop. His heart grew heavy with a feeling of resentment whenever he recalled those forgotten moments of his youth made up of a thousand yearnings, tears and pain.

Anupam tried to take hold of himself firmly and did not meet Anjali for the next few days, knowing full well that she would turn up at the weekly market clutching her Manipuri bag in the hope of meeting him there. But he remained firm. It was far better to dive deep into his memories and dreams rather than meet her in person.

He remembered the cheap kaleidoscope he had once bought at a fair in his childhood, and how the picture changed magically every time he turned it around. Each had a different colour scheme, formation and the patterns changed continuously. Perhaps love too was something like that and life itself was made up of a few pieces of coloured glass. Living meant just turning them around. The glasses were in varied colours—red, green, blue, yellow, violet, orange, each depicting a feeling, and the heart ran around them all. If you stopped suddenly in between, love would give your heart a gentle tug and the glasses would turn into multi-coloured clouds, raining dreams and splashing the viewer with colours. Another turn and the colours vanished, reducing them to ordinary pieces of coloured glass once again. There was just one thing that Anupam could not understand. Why did the things that had happened during his stay in Simla Street still have the power to overwhelm him? Why did each instance of pain still make him feel like a martyr?

"Bappa, please go to the weekly market today. I don't feel like going," said Anupam. He felt amused to see Bappa's expression. How well he knew that age! Perhaps he had been planning a trip with Jhumjhum that morning. They would be sitting somewhere quiet and—Anupam wasn't sure about that! He looked at Bappa's face carefully, trying to understand how he felt. Perhaps Bappa did not yet understand what "love" actually is. Or perhaps this generation took things too casually and there was no place for softer feelings in its scheme!

"Maa, tell me quickly what I have to get from the market," said Bappa, looking annoyed. After he left, Anupam tried to imagine how Anjali would arrive at the market, bag in hand, her trim figure swinging rhythmically. She would look around for Anupam, wait eagerly for him to arrive. And then start for home with eyes smarting with unshed tears of disappointment. Then she would see Bappa and make her way to him. She would not be able to ask about him directly and simply say, "All well at home, Bappa?" Anupam relished her possible anxiety as he imagined the whole scene.

For all these years Anupam did not know if Anjali remembered him or how she felt about him. He had no idea that his memory was so precious to her. The knowledge made him feel proud. But now the pride had turned to restlessness. After all, he was a human being with human needs and desires. And more importantly, he was a man. He could not convince himself that Anjali's feelings for him were real unless he could also hold her in his arms. There was no other way of relieving the anguish he felt at times. That is why it sometimes seemed to him that all this was no more than a mere luxury to Anjali. Perhaps love itself was nothing more than a form of sport.

"They are terribly rich, aren't they?" Anita had asked after visiting their house for the first time. Anupam had not liked her remark and did not reply.

"Ranen babu's job must be a very well-paid one?" Anita had continued, "Did you notice the posh carpet and the furniture? I heard they are all gifts from his office. Jhumjhum mentioned that they have a car in their Calcutta house, also provided by the office." Anupam had tried to smile and said, "Well, obviously she has a better destiny! You were merely fated to marry a poor teacher." Anita was annoyed by the remark and left the place in a huff. What could Anupam do?

He felt that Anita was comparing him with Ranen. Perhaps Anjali herself did it as well.

"I cannot live without seeing you any more," Anjali had told him while returning from the market, her voice husky with feeling. "I must see you at least once every day. Promise me that you will make it possible. I don't want anything more." Anupam had felt happy at her innocent request. But the prospect of merely seeing her was far from satisfactory where his own feelings were concerned.

What did a woman want from life? Hadn't Anjali got it all—a handsome and caring husband, a charming daughter like Jhumjhum, a carefree life and more than enough money? In short, hadn't she managed to acquire happiness itself? Perhaps she wanted to introduce a spot of fresh colour into her monotonous life by looking back at memories. That is why she had pulled out an old record that had been gathering dust for twenty years and wanted to play it on her radiogram once again, just as her daughter Jhumjhum had done. The old and dusty record was none other than Anupam himself, who had been transformed into a melodious song by Anjali's magic touch.

Anjali, do you remember that rainy day at Simla Street? In summer the water supply would be badly hit and water flew in a thread-like stream from the taps. But the picture was completely different once monsoon arrived. The slightest shower would bring about waist-deep water—Thanthane Kalibari, Simla Street, Ramdulal Sarkar Street, Bethune Row would all be under water, bringing the trams and buses to a halt. On one such morning both you and I had to give college a miss as it had been raining incessantly since morning. You were on the terrace with your friends, running about and dancing in the rain with your arms raised, like a little child. Once you pulled the anchal of your sari and covered your head the way a married woman does, and looked at me with the corner of your eyes to see if I'd been watching your antics. Then all of you burst out laughing and put your arms round each other, whispering secrets. Water dripped from your forehead, face and your hair. Your wet sari clung to your body, revealing your arms and shoulders. The beauty of your figure, your bare neck, your breasts, your chin, lips and eyes struck my consciousness like a streak of lightning as I felt an unbearable agony in my heart. As I stood on our balcony looking at you, I felt the touch and smell of rain on my face. The terrace of our house did not belong to us but I would go up in the rain sometimes. That morning as I felt the raindrops on my face, I was conscious that we were both being drenched in the same rain, the same rain was touching us both at the same time.

Anjali had shared yet another memory with him that afternoon. "Do you remember that afternoon during a torrid summer when our house had no water supply?"

"Yes, and you had called out to my mother, saying, 'Aunty, there isn't a drop of water in our house. My brothers have all gone for a wash at the roadside tap. But what am I to do?'" replied Anupam.

"So you do remember? And aunty said, 'No problem. Come to our place and have a bath.'" Anjali burst out laughing. "Well, I did go to your house, my towel slung across my shoulder. When I came face to face with you on the stairs, I felt so nervous that I dropped my soap-case!" It was Anupam's turn to laugh as he said, "But I did not pick it up and give it back because I was so angry with you for not giving me a chance to speak, although you passed by me on the staircase."

Anjali had stopped walking and looked at him admiringly. "How well you remember! Isn't it marvellous? But I feel like laughing when I think how foolish I was then. I felt nervous to open the door even after my bath because I knew you would be somewhere around the staircase. My heart was thumping madly when I saw you and I just ran for my life. But I felt sorry the moment I returned home."

Yes, memories were nothing but old records. And Anjali merely wanted to hear them over and over again. It was nothing more than that. Just so that her cup of happiness might spill over! It was good to know that she had remembered him for all these years. But he wouldn't give in, however much she called him. He would stop himself because he was not eighteen any more and could no longer be satisfied by merely looking at her from afar. But he knew how an eighteen-year-old felt about love and was not apprehensive about Bappa. He had no wish to protect him the way Anita did. In fact, Anupam did not wish Bappa to spend his life hanging on to an empty dream. If Bappa really fell in love with Jhumjhum or if he felt like snatching a few dream moments from life, he was welcome to do it. Anupam would not mind.

Life before he had reached the age of twenty held no particular significance for Anupam. His father was an extremely orthodox man. And yet, Anupam realised, to his utter surprise, that his father had been no older than he was now himself at the time. Maybe just a year or two older. Why then did his father seem so old to him? Surely he wouldn't get to be like his father in another couple of years? People in his college did not consider Anupam to be old either. If they did, perhaps they would treat him more respectfully.

Anupam's mother used to keep herself busy with her thousand and one religious rituals. She still does. She did not approve of Anupam's lifestyle at all and considered it highly irregular. She was so annoyed at his holding his glass with his left hand instead of the right one during meals that she created a regular scene, walked out of his house and went to live with his brother Bilu. Anupam recalled that he used to be really scared of his mother even during his college days. In fact, he used to be afraid of his brother too. Bilu was aware of it and might have spoken about it to Anjali. Anupam used to be afraid at times that perhaps it was Bilu whom

Anjali really loved and not him. The thought hurt him so much that he tried his best not to think of her. The people of his locality respected his father and held him in great esteem. Anupam was afraid that if he tried to speak to Anjali, the incident might spoil his father's image.

Anupam was so lost in his thoughts that he started when Anita came into the room and said, "Ranen babu has sent a man with a note." She handed Anupam the slip of paper. Anupam looked up and saw Bipin, Ranen's servant. He had a duster on his shoulder, as usual. Anupam read the note and looked at Anita.

"We hardly ever go out," said Anita, "since they have asked us, why don't we go?"

Anupam thought for a moment. What should he tell Bipin in answer to the note? It was written on a piece of paper torn from an exercise book.

> Anita,
>
> My husband had promised to take Bappa and Jhumjhum to the Shurgi Hill and the Shankh River some time. We have managed to get hold of a jeep today. Why don't all of you come as well, we can spend an enjoyable afternoon together...
>
> Anjali

Spend an enjoyable afternoon together! Anupam had been firm with himself for the last few days. But his firmness broke down before such an appeal. He looked at Bipin, who was waiting for his reply, and said, "Very well. Please tell them that we shall go." Bipin went back. Anita returned to her work. Anupam picked up the note and read it again and again. Her handwriting looked familiar and he remembered that Anjali had once left a notebook of hers on Bilu's table, which he had examined carefully for a long time. He had wanted to see if there was anything about him and if she had left it behind deliberately.

Anupam could not destroy the slip of paper. He folded it and kept it in his pocket, as he would have done with something precious. A line from the note haunted him repeatedly—"spend an enjoyable afternoon together". It suddenly made him feel elated. He realised that if he didn't go, Anjali would feel his absence acutely and it would seem to her as though no one had come!

Chapter 11

ALL of them were ready by the time the jeep arrived and came out when they heard the honk. Jhumjhum waved her arm, shouting, "Hip, hip, hurray!" Ranen, seated beside the driver, smiled at her and alighted from the jeep. When he got up again, Bappa jumped up and sat next to him. Anupam smiled at his tactics. It was so typical of Bappa to somehow manage a seat by the window! Anupam sat behind with Anita, Anjali, Hasu and Jhumjhum.

"Aunty, you'd better hold on to Jhumjhum fast," said Bappa, as soon as the jeep started, "she is jumping about so much, she's sure to roll off the jeep when we go up the hill." Anjali burst out laughing at his words while Anita said, "Be quiet, will you?"

The jeep moved speedily towards the Santhal village of Kanialuka, on an uneven track that had deep trenches along the sides. The village stood at the far end of the mining settlement. The way up the Shurgi Hill was from the middle of this village. The path went up the hill, going round and round, and then went down again to the banks of the Shankh River.

Anita was looking really happy. Her life normally centred around household chores and the kitchen. This monotony was broken by an occasional walk or two; she had only been to Rakha once. So she heartily welcomed this chance of an outing. But Anjali did not enjoy exerting herself and said to her husband, "Mind you, I'll go just as far as this jeep does and not a step further!" Everyone burst out laughing at her words. "I am so glad to have a little change," said Anita, "life was really getting too monotonous."

Monotonous? Anupam asked himself. Was their life really monotonous?

Well, what else could one call a life bereft of variety? It was even more so when he was young. Life was one dreary round of studying, taking on a job, getting married—all part of a set routine. Even love, for that matter. Here was Anjali right before his eyes, stealing a glance at him off and on—this was also part of the same routine. Anita was quite right. Anupam said, "Yes, there is really no variety in our life. You know, Ranen babu, I often feel that life is nothing but a conducted tour doing the same rounds over and over again." Ranen, sitting silently all this time, merely nodded. Then all of a sudden he sighed and said, "But sometimes the routine conducted tour gets involved in a terrible accident." Anupam started. His heart skipped a beat as he tried to analyse the implication of his words. Anjali looked at her husband's face and then at Anupam.

Ranen burst out laughing. But the laughter had a note of uncertainty and sadness about it as he said, "And who knows when that accident might actually happen? So I thought that since I had promised Bappa and Jhumjhum that I would take them to see the Shurgi Hill..."

Anjali interrupted him, saying, "Please don't talk of accidents!" and gave her husband a scared look. The jeep was climbing uphill steadily.

Ranen spoke to Bappa in spurts. "Can you see that greenish layer of rocks? It is kainite." Or, "Bappa, can you tell me how much rock-phosphate that yellowish clay over there contains?"

Jhumjhum laughed and said, "Baba, please give up on your geology lessons and see how gorgeous the hill looks from here." Everyone turned back and gazed at the hilly slope. It was really a beautiful sight. The stony path looked like a bow with slopes of green fields on either side. They were wild paddy, janar and mustard—green, red and yellow. There was black paddy too and a snow-white grain that looked like cotton. It looked as if someone had spread out a colourful sari to dry.

Ranen spoke again. "You see there, those are all wild varieties of paddy. Have you ever seen black and red paddy before?" Anjali and Anupam looked at each other and smiled.

The top of the hill was flat like a plateau and there was no proper summit. It had a few clusters of Santhal cottages scattered here and there—clean and trim huts made of mud, some of them with small kitchen gardens. Their jeep moved fast and steadily, clearing one slope after another. There were thick, deep forests on both sides of the road. After sometime they saw the Sankh River far away, its water gleaming in the sun. Ranen had been sitting silently for a long time. He suddenly said, "Anupam babu, you were quite right. Life is a conducted tour." Anupam guessed that Ranen had been thinking of his chance remark all this time. Perhaps that was why he had been so silent.

Ranen spoke again. "I too had regarded life the same way. But sometimes an accident occurs because of a small mistake. Weren't you speaking of the lack of variety and change? Well, the change, if and when it happens, makes us realise how helpless we actually are."

"Don't start all that again," said Anjali in a complaining voice. Just then their jeep cleared the forests and stood before the banks of the river. The sun was shining through a crisp, cold and misty morning. "Lovely!" cried Jhumjhum in an ecstatic voice.

Jhumjhum was the first to jump down as soon as the jeep came to a halt. As soon as Bappa got down, she said, "Come on, Bappa, race me to the river. Let's see who can touch the water first." She ran down towards the river, followed by Bappa. Hasu tried to run behind them. But she stopped midway, gave them a look and turned back.

"I am tired," said Ranen and walked towards a tree. Then he sat down and leaned against it. Anupam and Anjali were also walking towards the river.

"It's not fair that Ranen babu should sit here all alone," said Anita. She stopped and said, "Come, Hasu, let's go and sit with him."

Anita and Hasu walked towards Ranen.

Anjali saw that Jhumjhum and Bappa had already reached the river and were sitting on the sand, laughing at each other. Then Bappa spread out his legs and lay down on the sand. Anjali smiled at their antics and then smiled at Anupam. Anupam returned the smile.

"Would you mind if they manage to achieve what we failed to do?" asked Anjali.

Anupam smiled at her words. "I don't understand their generation, however much I try," he said. "I only know that they are extremely lucky. They don't have to throttle their heart's desire the way we were compelled to do."

"I don't think it's a question of luck at all," said Anjali. "This generation is swift at making friends, nothing more. They have no idea about love. I sometimes wonder why it is so."

"I can't blame them, whatever they do," said Anupam in a deep voice. "Perhaps I always wanted that Bappa should be able to achieve what I myself couldn't."

"Perhaps you are right," said Anjali, looking tenderly at Jhumjhum and Bappa. "Don't they look nice together?"

Anupam did not reply. He realised that Anjali was building castles in the air about Jhumjhum and Bappa. But he also felt a strange apprehension about the relationship.

Anupam took off his shoes and waded into the river and splashed some water on his face. How deliciously cold the water felt! Then both of them turned back and walked towards the others.

"You haven't been to the market lately!" said Anjali to Anupam, "I was looking for you all over the place today."

Anupam looked steadily at Anjali. "What's the use? It merely adds to my pain."

"You know, I couldn't sleep at all last night," said Anjali. "If I could, I might have dreamed of you."

Anupam burst out laughing.

"During those days you studied for a long time at night. Then you would come and stand in the balcony. I went to bed only after that one last glimpse. I couldn't sleep without seeing you," said Anjali.

"I never put out the light in my room until you switched off yours," said Anupam. Anjali's glance was full of deep feeling.

"I knew the exact sound of your closing the door or opening the window," she said. "I knew that it couldn't be anyone else. I still remember the sound."

Anjali was sinking into memories as she walked back. Then she suddenly looked conscious and started moving towards the tree where Ranen, Anita and Hasu were seated. Suddenly Anupam said, "We don't have much time, Anjali. As it is, we are running short of time. I am tired of playing your childish game of *don't you remember* and find it quite unbearable. I want you, Anjali. I want you close to me. You and just you alone. Tell me when I can. You must tell me today." Anjali looked at Anupam in surprise. Anupam's whole body seemed to be trembling with intense feeling. The expression in his eyes had changed too.

Anjali said, "But I don't need anything. I never wanted anything more. I just want to see you."

There was a fierce note in Anupam's voice as he said, "I want to get rid of the accumulated thirst of twenty years. You have to agree, Anjali. You *must*."

Suddenly Anjali looked totally helpless and felt very weak.

"We are running short of time," said Anupam, once again.

Anjali looked at him with tragic eyes and then looked down. She had come to a standstill. "I no longer have the strength of mind to refuse you," she said softly. Her words seemed to be drenched in tears. Anupam's heart was aglow with ecstasy. Anjali whispered something in a low voice and Anupam agreed. Wednesday! The single word, denoting a particular date, set free the music in his heart. Both of them walked fast. Perhaps both felt too excited to amble as they had been doing. Anupam turned and looked at Bappa and Jhumjhum once again. He saw them sitting on the wet sand, building a sand castle. It was a huge castle. But it was made of sand.

Chapter 12

WEDNESDAY! The word echoed and re-echoed in Anjali's mind continuously. She could not stop herself from waiting eagerly for the day. Anupam's impassioned words, "I want you close to me and alone," had set her blood on fire, bringing on tremors within her whole body. Had this not been her own eager desire for the last twenty years too? Had she not told herself repeatedly, "I want you close and I want just you alone," deep down in her heart? She knew that it was true. That was why she had been so afraid of putting it into words. That was why she felt afraid when Anupam actually said it.

Despite being afraid, she had waited for this moment with baited breath, her entire being trembling with fear, joy and excitement. She had wanted to tell him, "No, no! I don't want this kind of earthy, sensual pleasure. Please forgive me and let me live with my loneliness." But she could not bring herself to say it. She could not hurt Anupam after all these years by refusing him now. She had tried to cry out, "I am sinking into the quicksand of sin, please save me! I had merely wanted to dream in my sleep…do not wake me up." But Anjali had not succeeded. She had not been able to control herself. She could not help wondering if she had been in a sinful existence all along or if she had just transgressed into one? But suddenly the words echoed within her heart—adulteress…unfaithful…a fallen woman! Had she been just that all this time? Or had she turned into one after that incident?

Isn't it true that I have been unfaithful to Ranen deep down in my heart for the last twenty years despite never having touched Anupam, even in my dreams? And isn't it equally true that Ranen has lived with my body for the last twenty years but has he ever been able to touch my heart? I had tried to find the man who lived in my memory within the man I acknowledged as my husband, every day and every moment of my life. So, why worry, Anjali? You have been unfaithful to your husband all along, sunk in your secret world of sin.

Anjali laughed unsteadily in the darkness of the night and tried to convince herself. Hadn't she loved the moments when Anupam had whispered to her, "Come close to me, close…even closer!"? Hadn't her whole being responded when he had pulled her into his arms, lifted her chin and kissed her? She had trembled visibly. A wonderful feeling of bliss mixed with fear, pain and excitement had brought tears to her eyes. Anupam felt the tears and said in a hushed voice, "Anjali, what's this? You're crying! I don't want anything! I don't want anything that pains you." Anjali had laughed wildly and said, "No, no, I'm not crying. Look at me, I am not crying." She had dried her eyes and looked up at him in the semi-darkness of the room. She could not see his face clearly. Neither could he. They merely made the attempt to look into each other's eyes, the faint light making everything indistinct.

As Anjali re-lived every moment of that afternoon, she tried to justify her action.

How much can you hurt me, Anupam? How much pain can you inflict on me today? I have hurt you far more in the past. My marriage was fixed all of a sudden and I wept the whole day. Every girl dreams of her wedding day with joy and waits for it eagerly. But I merely cried. I only remembered that someone had offered me his love but I had refused him every time.

"Anjali, you had hurt me badly and I have lived all these years carrying that pain in my heart," Anupam had told her. "But I shall spend the rest of my life with the memory of today's fulfilment."

"But you had given me a greater pain by letting me hurt you," said Anjali. "I had thought I would meet you once before tying the knot and beg for your forgiveness. I had wanted to gift you this day of fulfilment then itself—twenty years ago."

Anupam held Anjali tenderly in the semi-darkness as he kissed her cheeks, her lips, her eyes, her chin and her silky soft hair passionately and whispered, "I had run away because I was too weak to face the insult."

"Yes, I know. I looked for you everywhere without success," whispered Anjali, "My eyes sought you everywhere. Finally, I asked Bilu where you were and I broke into tears when he told me."

Anupam held her close to his heart, close enough to hear her heartbeat. Then he said, "I don't want to run away any more, Anjali. This bond between us will always keep us close to each other, no matter how far we are in reality."

"Always," Anjali had whispered ecstatically.

The entire episode had seemed like a beautiful dream to Anjali. After those moments of fulfilment, she felt as light as a cloud, as soft as a feather...floating into an unknown realm of bliss. She recalled and re-lived every moment the next day and remembered every word that Anupam had spoken. His touch seemed to embrace her entire self like an unspoken cloud of euphoria. She smiled rapturously as she stood before the mirror and saw the red streaks on her breasts.

Anjali was all alone at home at the time. Jhumjhum was out with her cycle. Bipin had gone to the teashop on the opposite side of the road to play cards. That was how he spent all his afternoons. For a moment she thought of her husband who was in his office. But thinking of him made her feel uncomfortable, which was also brought with it a feeling of remorse. Last night as she lay next to him in bed, this same feeling had pervaded her, making her wince again and again. The distance between them was actually less than a foot but she had felt that she was miles away from him. She remembered it as she stood before the mirror.

Just at that moment, Anjali heard a commotion outside the gate. She had never for a moment imagined that disaster could strike her life at this moment of enchantment. But the noise prompted her to go out towards the gate, feeling worried and anxious, as she saw the crowd outside. "It's nothing, nothing to worry about, Ranen babu just felt giddy for a moment and had fallen down in the office," one of the men told Anjali as he noticed her approaching them. Anjali rushed to the waiting car and asked, "What's wrong? What has happened?" Three or four men helped Ranen get down from the car. But he stopped them and staggered inside the house himself and fell into his bed.

"He was feeling dizzy," said one of the men. Another one said, "We have already informed the doctor. He must be on his way."

Strangely enough, although this very man had seemed miles distant last night, Anjali clung to him right now as tears ran down her cheeks.

"Tell me what's wrong and where exactly is it paining?" pleaded Anjali with tears in her eyes, "Don't keep quiet, please, I beg of you." She unbuttoned his shirt and stroked his chest. Ranen looked at her, his eyes full of mute suffering. But he did not speak. He tried to hold Anjali's hand, which lay on his chest. But though he lifted her hand in an attempt to take it in his own, he could not do it. Anjali saw two drops of tears gleaming at the corner of his eyes. They rolled down his cheeks as soon as he closed his eyes. Anjali brushed them off with her soft fingers and wiped off her own eyes with her *anchal.*

Chapter 13

JHUMJHUM had fallen asleep. She found nothing to do in the afternoons so she spent the time turning over the pages of magazines or reading a storybook. She had been reading one when she fell asleep. But the commotion outside the gate woke her up. At first she could make out nothing and was merely surprised to see so many people from her father's office in the house. Then she saw her father lying in bed and looked at her mother's face. But she could not bring herself to ask any questions.

Just then Bappa came running inside the room, hot and breathless. He had heard about Ranen from someone outside the gate. "What's wrong, Aunty?" he asked Anjali in a worried voice, still panting. Anjali looked at him with distressed eyes and replied, "I don't know."

"What about the doctor? Have you called Dr Sen yet?" asked Bappa, looking at the group of office people. "I'd better go myself." He rushed out of the room, Jhumjhum following him with an anxious face. Bappa looked at her and tapped her shoulder gently. He wanted to assure her that all would be well. But he couldn't bring himself to say anything and just rushed out. Jhumjhum stood gazing at the departing figure, as long as he was visible, with a feeling of dependence in her heart. Then she came inside the room and stood quietly, holding on to the cot where her father lay, and looked intently at his face.

She wondered if he had suffered a stroke. She had heard the word many times and only had a vague idea of what it meant. Had it really happened to her father? She could not bring herself to ask anyone. She remembered that people often died of a stroke. Her friend's father had died because he had suffered one. When it happened, her jolly and happy-go-lucky friend had changed overnight, looking sad and serious all the time. Jhumjhum felt miserable when she thought how the incident had changed her friend's entire life.

In a little while there was the sound of a car stopping at the gate. Everyone rushed out to see who it was, including Jhumjhum. She saw Bappa getting down from the car, followed by the doctor. Bappa carried the doctor's bag and showed him the way. Anjali was still sitting quietly beside her husband. She gave the doctor a tragic, appealing look and got up from her place. Everyone was quiet. As the doctor examined his patient, he wanted to know what exactly had happened. One of the men present in the room said that he had fallen down in the office as he suddenly felt unsteady. The doctor examined him carefully for a long time and gave them a smile of assurance. "It is nothing to be worried about," he told them. He gave Ranen a shot and wrote out a prescription. "You won't get this medicine here," he said, "someone must go to Jamshedpur to fetch it."

"I'll go," said Bappa at once. Jhumjhum looked at Bappa, her face aglow with relief and gratitude.

"Could anyone tell me when is the next train to Jamshedpur?" asked Bappa.

One of the men said, "You could also go by bus and change at Haludpukur."

Anjali got up when she heard Bappa. She brought out her purse and gave it to Jhumjhum. All her money, her home, her expensive furniture and everything else she possessed seemed to have become meaningless all of a sudden. There was just one person who really mattered and it was her husband. Her eyes could see nothing but his ailing body.

One by one the people from Ranen's office left the place. So did the doctor. One of the men called out to Anjali and said, "Please don't hesitate to call us if you need anything. And don't worry."

Suddenly the room seemed strangely empty.

Anjali bent down close to her husband's face and asked, "Do you have any pain?"

Bappa went out of the room, followed by Jhumjhum. He turned to her and said, "Jhumjhum, when Bipin da comes home..."

"You don't have to tell me," said Jhumjhum. "Don't worry. I'll go myself and tell your parents everything." Bappa left immediately, taking long strides in order to walk faster. Jhumjhum looked at him and felt that Bappa had grown up quite suddenly—from a boy into a man one could depend on.

Anupam and Anita arrived there soon after hearing the news.

"You should have sent for us at once, Anjali," said Anupam in a complaining voice.

Anjali did not reply. She could not meet Anupam's eyes. A storm of doubt and distaste raged within her heart. She heartily wished Anupam would leave the place, leave her alone and stay out of her sight so that she might not be compelled to see him.

It was she who had told him, "I want to see you," "I must see you," "I can't do without seeing you," repeatedly in the past. "I just have to see you every day," she had told him time and again. But now a strong feeling of repulsion rose from the depths of her heart that seemed to scream loudly, "I *don't* want to see you...ever again! For God's sake, go out of my sight!"

Her face turned ashen as she recalled a scene of intimacy and memories of last evening flashed within her consciousness. "I did not really wish to sink into sin," she told herself, "I merely wanted to revive old memories." Anjali could not bring herself to look at Anupam, as she battled fiercely with feelings of anger, annoyance and shame that raged within her, which she tried best to hide. She sat beside her husband as quietly as a statue and did not move to look at them even when Anupam and Anita came in. After what seemed hours, Anjali said to Anupam, "I think you should leave now. It is quite late already." The words sounded empty and formal, spoken without any feeling. Or was there a poisoned dart concealed in the words?

Anupam did not move. He saw Anjali tenderly sponging her husband's brow with a wet towel. Then she asked him something in a whisper and fetched some warm milk for him and fed him, little by little. A gentle, helpless kind of innocence gleamed on Anjali's face, the like of which Anupam had never seen before. He suddenly felt that she had grown very distant from him. He realised that his desire to be closer to Anjali was only a physical one. But that moment of fulfilment had turned her into a total stranger instead.

Someone from Ranen's office came to see him. Anita asked Anjali, "Should I stay back for the night? I might be of some help since you are all alone."

"Even I could stay back," said Anupam, "I don't have..."

"There is no need," said Anjali before he could finish his sentence, "Bipin is here."

"And Bappa will be here soon," added Jhumjhum. "Perhaps Bappa could..."

Anjali was growing quite frantic, unable to put up with Anupam's presence any longer. She only wanted him to leave, to go out of the house and out of her sight. She turned to Anita and said, "I think you should make haste and go back home. After all, you have left Hasu there all alone." Finally, Anupam and Anita got up to leave. Anupam said, "Please send for us if there is any need." Anjali did not reply. But she felt cleaner as soon as Anupam was out of the house. As though the mirror of her conscience had been removed from her vision at last.

Now there were just the three of them in the room—Ranen, Anjali and Jhumjhum. The huge bedroom had a sofa set in a corner. A big pedestal lamp with a coloured silk shade threw a soft glow in the room, as gentle and mild as the moonlight. Jhumjhum sat quietly on the sofa with her feet up. The frisky, happy-go-lucky girl had suddenly turned unnaturally quiet.

"Anju," called Ranen in a soft voice. Anjali was seated next to him. She moved closer and asked, "Is there something you want to say?"

"Anju, I am not really ill." His words sounded like a sigh. Anjali laid her hand on his chest and said, "Yes, I know. But please be quiet, dear. Don't talk right now."

Ranen remained quiet for a few minutes. Then he took Anjali's hand in his own and said in a broken voice, "I had meant to tell you before...I had been trying for the last few days...but couldn't bring myself to do it..."

"Please be quiet now," said Anjali again in a tearful voice, "later on you can tell me whatever you want to. But now you need to be quiet."

"No, no, don't ask me to be quiet," there were tears in Ranen's voice too, "do let me speak. I was greatly worried for the last few days. And I was feeling badly insulted."

"Please stop, for God's sake," said Anjali, embracing Ranen in an attempt to make him stop talking, completely forgetting Jhumjhum's presence in the room.

But Ranen went on, "I have done you both grave injustice by thinking only of myself and my own self-respect."

"Don't worry," cried Anjali, "I won't let your self-respect suffer in any way."

For a few moments there was silence in the room. Then Ranen said, "I am not ill, Anju. I got to know that my company suffered a heavy loss amounting to quite a few lakhs because of a mistake that I had made."

Anjali stared at Ranen, taken aback by the totally unexpected news.

"What are you saying?" she cried, "Anyway, whatever it is, forget it for the moment. You need to be quiet now."

"No, I must finish what I was saying," said Ranen, trembling with suppressed feelings, "they were being so insulting to me that I just couldn't take it any more and tendered my resignation in a moment of heat. And they have accepted my resignation, Anju. There is no ground beneath my feet right now." Anjali stared at her husband in utter disbelief. Jhumjhum stood up from the sofa in silence. She too was stunned. She had never imagined a situation like this and could not take in all that it implied.

"What are you saying?" asked Anjali in a voice full of despair. She seemed to be in the middle of a bad dream. Surely her husband was merely delirious and was saying things that were not meant to be taken seriously? Her husband without a job? Without any ground beneath his feet? Anjali did not seem to understand what the words implied.

Just then they heard the sound of footsteps as someone walked up the gravel path from their gate. The sound brought Jhumjhum back to reality and she rushed outside. An icy air struck her like a blow as it enveloped her from all sides. She stood in front of the door and looked towards the gate. Yes, it was Bappa walking up from the gate, shivering in the intense cold. His advancing figure looked like a silhouette in the darkness. Poor boy, thought Jhumjhum as she blamed herself bitterly for not having given him a warm scarf when he had rushed out to fetch her father's medicines. She felt sorry for him, combined with a warmer feeling. But immediately she remembered her father's words, that there was no ground beneath his feet…nothing but emptiness!

Bappa walked fast and came up the steps to the verandah. Jhumjhum wanted to speak but the words got stuck in her throat. Seeing him walk up all this way, shivering pitifully in the bitter cold, Jhumjhum just rushed up to him and held him close like a warm cover as she broke into tears. She tried to speak but couldn't bring herself to say anything.

Chapter 14

THE next few days centred around Ranen's recent illness. Ranen was a little better now but Anjali seemed to have changed overnight. She felt like a pretty little ship with a broken mast that tossed about aimlessly in the ocean because it had lost sight of its harbour. Anupam had visited them several times during this period because he was under the impression that Ranen was seriously ill. He could not help feeling sorry for Anjali and wanted to be with her in order to share her pain at this hour of need. He had wanted Anjali to depend on him and entrust some of her responsibilities to him. But Anjali seemed to be avoiding him. Why? He had asked himself several times, not understanding what was prompting her to act so strangely. He had wanted to possess her because he loved her and wanted her to acknowledge it too. Wasn't physical intimacy an important part of love? Why couldn't Anjali understand that?

Anupam had no idea that he did not matter to Anjali any more. Anjali had wanted to dream about him once when she had a solid ground beneath her feet. But that ground was no longer there to support her. She no longer had a future. There was no place in her life for dreams any more. Nor could she look at Jhumjhum's face without feeling guilty, ever since she had surrendered herself to Anupam. Now total uncertainty stared her in the face and life held no assurance of any kind. She found herself unable to face anyone under the present circumstances. She was also convinced that memories were no more than an unimportant luxury. What she had actually loved all these years was the security provided by her husband—that feeling of security and her husband's love had been one and the same. Only the realisation had not dawned on her before! Nor had she realised before that this love was inseparably bound with Jhumjhum's future.

That her father had no job was something Jhumjhum could not fully comprehend even now. But whenever she looked at her father's or her mother's face, she could sense that some terrible disaster had struck their lives.

Bappa was always around during this terrible time. He was always there, ready to do anything for any of them. Jhumjhum kept remembering that terrible winter night when Bappa had returned with the medicine, dead tired and shivering in the bitter cold. The very thought of Bappa brought on an unbearable ache within her heart.

That evening Bappa suddenly said, "Jhumjhum, you've been sitting at home with a serious face all this time. I only hope you don't fall ill yourself." Anjali heard him and looked at Jhumjhum. Then she said, "Jhumjhum, why don't both of you go out for a walk? You haven't left the house once for the last few days." Bappa also looked at Jhumjhum. Jhumjhum got up silently, changed her clothes and came back. "Let's go," she said to Bappa.

The soft sunlight of the winter afternoon gently touched both of them as they walked. They were on the lonely road that led to the Rakha mines, with trees and moss-covered walls of empty houses on either side. Jhumjhum came to a sudden halt and said, "Didn't I tell you the other day that I don't feel like thinking of anything or anyone in particular?"

"Yes, you did. But you are unnecessarily worrying about your father all the time," said Bappa. "Why? He is much better now, almost fully recovered."

Suddenly Jhumjhum burst into tears and looked at Bappa. Bappa saw that her eyes were brimming with tears. Lifting her tearful eyes to Bappa's, she said, "You don't understand anything! I have been thinking of you and only you all this time! I made several desperate attempts not to think of you but I ended up remembering you all the more." Bappa looked at her face in surprise and his own face lit up in joy. "Really? Do you really mean it, Jhumjhum?"

Jhumjhum looked at him steadily. "Tell me, did you ever think of me? You have merely been doing your duty like a good boy! I couldn't sleep the whole night because you wanted to keep awake. You returned home shivering in the cold that night so I threw off all my warm clothes so that I might share your pain."

"I have wanted to tell you a good many things but I didn't have the courage," said Bappa softly. "I was afraid you would treat my words as a joke. You know, I see your face whenever I close my eyes, Jhumjhum."

Jhumjhum laughed despite the tears in her eyes. They were standing in the shade of the broken wall, away from the main road. A Santhal boy walked past them, playing on his flute.

"Your eyes are full of tears, Jhumjhum," said Bappa. "Wipe your tears."

Jhumjhum looked down and whispered, "You wipe them for me."

Bappa stood there for a while, wondering what to do.

Jhumjhum repeated, "You wipe them for me. You must always wipe away my tears. All the time." Bappa drew her into his arms and gently kissed away the tears from her eyes. Suddenly Jhumjhum felt very shy. She lowered her face and started walking. Bappa was also feeling shy and tried to cover it up by saying, "Aunty is alone at home. If she suddenly needs something..."

Jhumjhum gave him a sidelong glance, smiled and said, "All you can think of is duty and more duty! Doctors, medicines, injections, fruits...Really, you remind me of a clock sometimes."

Bappa stretched out his hand and held hers in his own. "But *you* are there in all the things I think of! The entire clock is full of just you alone."

"I can rarely express my thoughts so beautifully," said Jhumjhum.

"But your eyes do," said Bappa. "What they tell me is even more beautiful."

Jhumjhum lifted her big eyes and said, "If you like my eyes so much, why don't you take them?"

"Not merely your eyes, I have already taken the whole of you in my camera," said Bappa.

"When?" asked Jhumjhum, surprised, "And where? On the day we had gone out to take photos?"

"No," said Bappa, smiling at her, "on the day I saw you for the first time. The evening you had come to our house with your cycle."

"I never saw you with a camera that evening," protested Jhumjhum, "Had you been hiding it?"

Bappa tapped his breast and said, "I have my camera right here."

Jhumjhum felt happy to hear his words. Her heart suddenly felt as soft as the green grass drenched in dew.

"But is your photo a permanent one?" asked Jhumjhum. "Can you promise that it will remain forever? Or will it fade into oblivion the moment you reach Calcutta?"

They walked past another mossy wall and heard the voices of a crowd of Santhal men and women walking on the other side. A group of young Santhal girls holding on to each other by the waist passed them by, laughing. Bappa looked at them and asked Jhumjhum, "You must tell me if I'll have to live with a mere picture all my life."

Jhumjhum laughed at his question. "You still can't believe me?"

There was a clean patch of grass right in front of them. Bappa suddenly sat down there, drawing his knees close to his chest. Jhumjhum waited for a while and then she too sat down facing him, her arms embracing his knees, her chin resting upon them, her face aglow with a naughty smile, and her eyes fixed in a steady gaze upon Bappa.

"What are you looking at?" Bappa asked her.

He felt slightly embarrassed but liked the way Jhumjhum sat leaning on him.

"Listen to me," said Jhumjhum.

"Tell me," said Bappa.

"Come closer," whispered Jhumjhum. Bappa brought his face close to hers and said, "Tell me now."

"Come closer still," said Jhumjhum.

Bappa smiled and obeyed her. Jhumjhum gently laid her cheek against his. Just then Bappa held her face with both his hands and kissed her on the forehead.

Both of them sat in silence while Jhumjhum moved a little. For a while they were both lost in thoughts, full of an unspoken happiness. Bappa pulled out a blade of grass. He bit one end of the grass and touched Jhumjhum's face with the other. Jhumjhum too held the other end between her teeth. After a while, she said, "Have you forgotten that we have to return home?"

"I wish we could sit here like this forever," said Bappa.

They got up slowly and started walking homeward. Jhumjhum suddenly said, "I don't like keeping secrets from you. But I don't want to say anything to spoil a beautiful day like this." Bappa did not ask her what the secret was. He merely said, "Today is the most beautiful day of my life."

Chapter 15

Despite his recovery, Ranen was swamped by a feeling of gloom and hopelessness. He tried his best to shake it off but did not succeed. It seemed impossible to stand up on his own feet any more. Although he never expressed it, he had been really proud of his job. It was only now that he realised on what a flimsy base his personality had rested all these years. He remembered attending a wedding in a relative's house only the other day where one of his aunts had been present. Despite her advanced years, she still doted on him as she did when he was a young boy. She had said amidst a roomful of people, "Ranu, dear, you are so high up in your job right now. I feel so proud when people speak of your grand position and achievements. But must you forget your old aunt just because you are a big shot now? Why don't you visit me any more?" The people in the room had cast admiring glances at him and someone asked the old lady who he was. "It's Ranen. Our own Ranu," his aunt had replied proudly. Ranen felt gratified by their obvious admiration and had felt immensely proud of himself.

Only the other day when they were in the club he had said to Gupta, "Kapoor may own the company but I am the one who holds the key!" Even then a cold war had been raging between Kapoor and himself. All this had happened just a short while ago and now he was a mere nobody! Wasn't it strange, thought Ranen, that his value should depend on a job, a solid, high-salaried job and the assurance of receiving a fat salary cheque at the end of the month! He had been valuable because of the knowledge that he was loaded! He had never imagined that so much, or rather, everything depended on it! Supposing he were to meet the same aunt today and she asked him, "I hear you have lost your job, Ranu? Is it really true?" What would he reply? Or if Gupta got to know about it and came to ask him if it was true? How would he answer him after the way he had bragged? Was security inevitably followed by insecurity in life?

Several uncertainties crept in to Ranen's mind. It made him wonder if it would have been better for everybody if he hadn't shot up to the top quite so fast. He had risen from one post to the next very rapidly during the last few years and his salary had increased in proportion. He had got used to a life of luxury and rash spending without building up a wall of security first. Or a solid provident fund to fall back upon. This was what made him feel so upset. He used to earn merely three hundred rupees when he first took up this job a few years ago. It would not have been difficult to find another job with the same salary today nor would he have felt that he had lost his self-respect.

Yes, he had made a huge mistake! He should never have handed in his resignation. Had it only been possible, he would have taken it back even now. It would merely mean having to face some digs and jeers if he did. But it was nothing compared to what he had lost. Most of the people in his office wouldn't even have known about it. Now he felt that he had suddenly become the laughing stock of his entire office. He was unable to meet Anjali's eyes and felt really afraid to look at Jhumjhum. It was a hard pill to swallow. It was money, just money! It all depended on how much one earned, thought Ranen. Otherwise, why couldn't he lift his head up proudly today and proclaim to the world and his wife, "Self-respect matters more than anything else, Anju! I just couldn't compromise with it for the sake of money." But instead of saying it he had asked her in a whisper, "Anju, does anyone else know about it? Has anyone heard what actually happened?"

Anjali cast a quick glance around her. No, Bipin was nowhere near. Then she asked in an equally low voice, "Whom do you mean?"

"Anupam babu and his family? Have they guessed anything?"

"No. No one knows anything or guesses the truth. So please don't say anything to anyone. I have also forbidden Jhumjhum to speak about it."

Ranen laid his head on his hands. How strange that he should care about what Anupam thought! He had been a perfect stranger even a few days ago. Probably he would never meet him again once they returned to Calcutta. And yet he felt so ashamed at the thought of his knowing what had actually happened.

Ranen was silent for a while and looked at Anjali's face. Then he said in a comforting voice, "Don't worry, Anju. I'll find another job. But you may have to face a tough time for a few months."

"I am not afraid of facing difficulties," said Anjali. But her words sounded hollow and did not carry conviction.

Ranen was seated in the easy chair, his head bent. Anjali, who had been standing all this time, now sat on the arm-rest of the chair. She stroked his hair gently and said, "Please don't lose heart."

"No, I won't," said Ranen, "but I am worried about Jhumjhum's future. I have just a few thousands in my provident fund. It's not much. After all, I got the big raise not too long ago. I think we ought to economise a bit until I find a new job. What do you say?"

"Of course," said Anjali. "Don't worry, I shall manage."

"To start with, we must shift to a cheaper and smaller flat when we return to Calcutta."

"When do we return?" Anjali asked. She was dying to get away from this place. "There's no point in hanging on here, is there?" She did not remember that only a few days ago this same Musabani-Rakha-Haludpukur had seemed so dear and attractive to her! She had roamed around to her heart's content, discovering beautiful places. And now the same places had lost their charm. There was no colour in the sky, no fragrance in the breeze. Everything was dull and drab. The only way to be free was to get away from here somehow.

Anjali had spent the last twenty years dreaming of her first love, the love of her youth. Anupam's thoughts and memories had been as true as the pole star in her life. For Anjali, life without Anupam seemed one big void and nothing else. Then Anupam had walked into her life once again like a bolt from the blue. She was just beginning to think herself the happiest woman on earth when this new disaster struck her life. She had been totally estranged from her husband for a brief spell when Anupam appeared in her life a second time. But now she suddenly discovered that it was her estranged husband who had actually been the closest to her heart. Did sin and virtue actually exist in life? Did they mean anything? Anjali asked herself and felt a wave of regret. Was Anupam responsible for the sudden change in her circumstances? Or was it she herself who was responsible? Did this catastrophe happen as the direct consequence of her sin? No, she simply would not believe in such superstition! But her heart ached because she had betrayed her husband's implicit trust.

"Please don't ask for more," Anjali had implored when Anupam touched her tenderly with both his hands like a blind man and had kissed her passionately on her lips, cheeks, eyes and her brow. Anupam had respected her wishes and had not insisted on more than she was prepared to give. But now Anjali was amazed to discover that her heart was totally empty, that she did not have any feelings left for Anupam! Seeing him made her feel uncomfortable now. His very presence seemed unbearable. She merely wanted to be left alone with her own thoughts and problems. And yet, she had told Anupam just the other day, "There is nothing that I cannot confide in you." She had spoken to him frankly about the ups and downs in her life. She had told him all about her problems in great details and had said repeatedly, "I have absolutely nothing to hide from you."

And now she felt like laughing at her past behaviour. At this moment, all she wanted was that Anupam should not know anything about her current situation and wanted to hide everything from him. She glanced at the things around her—her furniture and other accessories. The expensive carpet on the floor, the elegant sofa set, the exclusive curtains, the bed and wardrobe. All these years she had measured her own value by the value of the things she owned. She was what she possessed. But now she could no longer do that because she was no longer an individual entity. She was now part of her husband's world that had been struck by disaster. She was part of him now, the way she had been long ago when Jhumjhum was critically ill. They had been together in their anxiety, pain and distress, each comforting the other, seeking strength from one another. They had cried together when things grew really serious and shared the same relief and joy when Jhumjhum eventually turned the corner and recovered.

Ranen broke the silence after a little while. "Perhaps Jhumjhum might feel ashamed to meet her old friends for some time, until things are settled. But it will not be for more than a few months. I shall be up on my feet once again, you'll see."

"Please don't worry," said Anjali. "Jhumjhum is no longer a child. She will understand." But Anjali knew that these were mere words. Her heart still floated willy-nilly in a world of uncertainty.

But she was determined about one thing—she would play the queen to the hilt before leaving this place. A queen who had nothing more to wish for!

"Weren't you planning to call Anupam babu's family to dinner?" Ranen remarked suddenly. Anjali grabbed the opportunity. All these days she had projected herself to Anupam as a tragic, lovelorn woman, bereft of true love, living on memories and pining all alone. But this time he should see her in a totally different light.

She re-decorated all the rooms differently, changing all the curtains. Then she ordered an exclusive menu and sent Bipin to fetch the things from Haludpukur. She had sent for *mishit doi* (sweet yoghurt) in the morning itself and had it stored in the fridge. Then she spent the entire afternoon cooking *payesh* (a special kind of rice pudding) because Anupam loved it. She remembered how his mother would make it for him on his birthday, feeding it to him herself. She also remembered his other favourites—curry of *magur* fish (catfish), for one. As it was not readily available, she had got a Santhal girl to fetch some from the distant Kanialuka village. She did not want him to suspect that he now meant nothing to her.

Anupam arrived with his family in the evening. Anjali looked at him and laughed in her heart of hearts. The poor man had no idea that he was now totally redundant so far as she was concerned. He had imagined that physical intimacy meant acceptance! Perhaps he had felt that possessing her body would mean a total possession of her soul as well, a bond that nothing could destroy. And now he had lost both body and soul…forever!

Anita had dressed up with unusual care that evening. She was wearing a thick cluster of bangles and an expensive necklace. Perhaps she had been feeling inferior to Anjali all these days after seeing her affluence and wanted to bridge the gap by dressing as well as she could. Anita had no idea that Anjali's valuable possessions had lost all their value under her present circumstances. Anjali played the role she had selected to perfection that entire evening, with Anupam and his family as the audience. It was the role of a happy, contented and totally fulfilled wife who wanted nothing more from life. She behaved as though nothing had changed for her and everything was exactly what it had been before the disaster. She spoke non-stop, bubbling over with laughter every now and then, giving the impression that she was unable to contain her happiness within herself.

"Jhumjhum, why don't you sing a song for uncle and aunty?" she had said in an excited voice, "Really, I don't know how many other plans her father has made for her! She has two professors who come home to teach her in Calcutta and a music teacher..."

"Please stop it, Maa," said Jhumjhum, cutting her short as she lifted her eyes from the plate.

"Why should I stop?" asked Anjali in an affected voice. "Isn't it a fact that we spend more than three hundred rupees every month for you alone? Can you guess how much she spends on her clothes alone, Anita? And all because she has always been her father's darling, the apple of his eyes!"

For a moment no one spoke. Then Anjali said, "We are leaving, you know. Ranen's office wants him back in Calcutta and has asked him to be quick about it." Anupam looked at the dining table with its milk-white cover and the tastefully arranged flower vase at the centre. Anjali loved flowers and was an expert where flower arrangements were concerned.

"So, you are leaving?" asked Anupam, not knowing what else to say, "When?"

Anjali stood up swaying her body in a playful rhythm as she said in a happy and excited voice, "I'll tell you all about it. But before that, please have a little more chicken. I know you love it."

As she stood looking at the table, she continued to sway her body rhythmically which seemed to spell her deep content with life. She looked much less than her actual age as she tried to appear as thrilled and overjoyed as a young girl. After a few moments she pulled her chair back and sat down at the table. "I may as well tell you the good news," she said, "Ranen has been offered another big promotion."

Anita looked at her husband's face. "Is that so?" she said to Anjali.

"That's great!" said Anupam, trying to smile. Anjali was satisfied. She could plainly see that the news had not made Anupam happy at all and that was just what she wanted.

It was I who made you proud of yourself by telling you repeatedly how much I cared for you and now I myself shall shatter that pride!

Anjali turned to Anita. "Anita, you are not eating anything at all. You ought to eat double share of everything since today is such a special day for us!" Anjali burst out laughing loudly as though she had said something really amusing. She stood up once again. Then she walked up to the radiogram swaying rhythmically with dance-like steps, her expensive chiffon sari blowing in the breeze, spreading whiffs of her exotic imported perfume on all sides. She switched on the radiogram, filling the room with loud music. "Well, I've told you the great news already," she said, "Ranen has been selected for something really special." And Ranen smiled in agreement.

Jhumjhum alone was astonished by her mother's behaviour. She had never seen her behaving like this before. As a matter of fact, she had always felt that despite having everything her mother could not appreciate it fully, rather like a full-grown lotus that refused to bloom and spread out its petals. She remembered she had once said to a classmate of hers, "You know, my mother simply does not know how to enjoy life."

But Anjali was quite determined to play the role of an ecstatic and fulfilled wife the entire evening. All these days she had pretended to be a lovelorn and unhappy woman who only wanted to tell the lover of her youth, "I want to see you, I long to see you every day" or "my dreams are still filled with you." But now that there was no solid ground beneath her feet she wanted to pretend that she was actually seated on a golden throne from where she could barely notice his existence.

Anjali's school friend Bina had once come to look her up after she was married. After seeing her beautiful home and her lavish and expensive lifestyle, Bina had remarked, "Anjali, you are the only one among our friends who is really happy." Anjali had smiled and replied, "You are quite wrong, you know. I don't really care for wealth. You know all about me and my past. I don't think anything can be of real value if one is parted from one's love." Bina had said, "All of us live in hope, dreaming of things that might come to us some day. But life has already given you everything and you have nothing left to wish for. That is why you are going around looking for sorrow." Perhaps Bina had spoken the actual truth that evening, thought Anjali. Right now she did not feel the slightest pain for the unfulfilled love of her youth! She could only see the terrible future gaping at her.

Anjali turned to her husband. She gave him a tender look and said in a voice full of love, "Please don't sit there looking so glum. You ought to feel the happiest and proudest amongst us all." Ranen tried to smile. He was well aware that Anjali was playing her part with grim determination and would continue to play it till the end of the party. It was a mystery how she could keep it up for so long!

Anupam had never seen her look or act so happy during his entire visit. She seemed like a total stranger to him this evening—a stranger who sat on a throne like a goddess, proudly receiving prayers! Anupam tried to hide the pain within his heart and smiled broadly as he said, "Well, don't forget us after reaching your exalted position, will you? What do you say, Jhumjhum? I hope you will remember us after you return to Calcutta?" Anjali knew that the words were actually meant for her. But Jhumjhum could not smile and kept her eyes fixed on her plate.

Anjali looked at Ranen once again. "Didn't you say that you would throw a huge party to celebrate your new position after we return? I am *really* going to dress up that night, I warn you." Anita burst out laughing. Anupam joined her in the laughter, feeling amused at Anjali's childish joy at the thought of dressing up.

"Why are you all laughing?" asked Anjali. Looking at Jhumjhum she continued, "Obviously my days of dressing up are numbered with Jhumjhum growing up so fast! We shall soon have a foreign-returned, handsome young man, a covenanted officer in some big firm, pursuing her and asking for her hand. I'd like that really well because I don't care two hoots for the IAS officers of today." Jhumjhum had been eating silently with her head bent over her plate, trying not to react to her mother's unusual performance. But she could not take it any more and screamed rudely, "Shut up, Maa! Shut up, for God's sake!" She stood up, pushing the chair noisily. Anjali, Anita and Anupam stared at her in surprise and saw that Jhumjhum's eyes were full of tears. But she left the room abruptly before anyone could say anything.

A grim hush filled the room. As though everything had been stunned to silence. Suddenly Anupam noticed that the same record was playing in the radiogram over and over again. Anupam looked at Bappa. Bappa was looking down too, his face looking ashen in the light. He looked insulted and stricken with shame. A strange pain gnawed within Anupam's heart. His heart went out to Bappa in sympathy, weeping silent tears. As Anupam looked at his son's face, he said to himself: *So you too have tasted death just the way I did! I never imagined for a moment that you too would be a fool, just the way I had been, and fall in love! I had thought that you belonged to a different generation, practical and tough, well able to shake off the thorns of disappointment from your heart.*

Anjali, do you remember that one day, a long time ago, my face looked just as stricken and ashen as Bappa's face looks today? Surely you can't have forgotten? There was a function at your college that day. I had dropped in and had asked a girl whom I knew to call you. But you had thrown her out, saying, 'Tell him to go away and to leave immediately. I don't wish to see him!' Anjali, the insult of those words spoken by you was written all over my face and I didn't know where to hide it. I felt too ashamed to face the girl through whom I had sent you that message. Anjali, did you realise that from that moment I had never looked into your eyes again? When you met me here you made light of the incident and told me that you had sent that message because you were too nervous at the thought of really meeting me, that you were embarrassed! Anjali, are you aware that you did not succeed in wiping off the bitter memory of that afternoon even when you surrendered yourself to me? That innocent youth who had offered nothing but the purest love could never look up again for the rest of his life because of your insult? That he felt a sense of void which nothing could fill up?"

Anupam's heart addressed the next message to Bappa, saying in his heart: *Bappa, I was wrong! People are the same no matter what age they belong to. That is why you made the same mistake as I did—you have lost your heart. You are trying to hide the fact from us today and you will have to continue hiding the fact all your life.*

Anjali wasn't through with her play-acting and was determined to keep on until the end of the party. She was playing the role of a queen and meant to convince her audience that it was the reality. She laughed affectedly as Jhumjhum left the room and said, "Just look at that foolish girl! As if I'm getting her married to her officer right now! I know she wants to go to London first and we shall certainly wait until she returns."

Ranen laughed too. "Do you remember what Jhumjhum used to say when she was young?"

"Of course," said Anjali joining his laughter, "she always said, 'my husband should have two cars. One will be mine.'"

Bappa was feeling breathless by now. He got up silently from the table. "Aunty, I am leaving," he said. "I am feeling very sleepy."

Anjali did not even notice that he left the place without washing his hands.

Ranen said, "Bappa is a very good boy. It would have been a real problem if he hadn't been there to help us during those difficult days when I was ill."

Anupam said nothing in reply. He turned to Hasu and said, "Why didn't you also go home with your brother?" Hasu spoke little as a rule. Even now she made no reply to her father's query.

Anita felt extremely annoyed with the entire situation and found it quite unbearable right then. Jhumjhum's sudden screaming and leaving the room so abruptly, followed by Bappa's hasty departure, provided her with the key to the mystery. So it was just what she had feared! How disgraceful! She longed to rush home herself and give Bappa a tight slap on his cheek! Foolish boy!

"You haven't given me your address yet," said Anupam to Ranen as a matter of courtesy. He had no idea what prompted him to say it.

"What's the use of giving you the old address?" said Anjali at once. "We shall be shifting to a much bigger and better flat as soon as we are back. Why don't you leave your address with us instead?"

Anjali continued to play-act the rest of the evening, right until Anupam, Anita and Hasu got up to leave. Jhumjhum did not come out of her room at all. Not even to wish them goodbye.

Ranen informed Anupam and Anita, "We are leaving the day after tomorrow by the nine-fifteen train."

Finally the guests were out of the house. Immediately the room seemed full of a strange void, as blank as the sky. There seemed to be nothing but emptiness and hopelessness all around them. Anjali the actress seemed to taunt the actual Anjali. Ranen and Anjali remained seated in two distant corners of the room, unable to look at each other or speak a single word. They were not even able to meet each other's eyes. Anjali wanted to cry her heart out, although she did not know the reason behind it. Laying her head on the small table she burst into tears. Ranen stood up and walked up to her. "Get up, Anju dear, please don't cry," he said stroking her head gently. But Anjali continued to sob.

What had she done? She had not really wanted to hurt Anupam like this! She merely wanted to show him that she was now one with her husband. And she wanted Ranen to know that she supported him whole-heartedly. But she had no wish to banish Anupam from her memory forever. She knew that her current difficulties would be overcome some day and she would feel secure once again. But her memories were lost for good. She felt a lump of pain in her throat. Suddenly she stood up and raised her tearful eyes to her husband, saying in a shaky voice, "Please save me." Ranen laid both his hands on her shoulders and said in a voice full of deep feeling, "You have saved yourself, Anju."

Chapter 16

A BITTERLY cold air struck their faces as soon as Anupam, Anita and Hasu came out of the house. But Anupam forgot to pull out his shawl and cover his ears. Had it been some other time, Anita would have reminded him and said, "Do you want to catch a cold again? How can you be so careless?" But now she merely walked in grim silence. There was not a sound to be heard anywhere. There seemed to be nothing but a solid wall of darkness on all sides. A lone light shone from the distant hilltop belonging to Copper House. The rhythmic sound of the moving buckets had stopped quite some time ago and the ropeway stood still now. Anupam and Anita walked side by side without speaking a single word to each other for a long time. No one cared to break the spell of total silence, each lost in his and her own thoughts. Neither knew what exactly the other was thinking but both felt sure that they were thinking of the same thing. They suddenly felt very close to each other.

"Just see what you've done!" said Anita in a voice drenched in tears. "Why did you tell me that this generation is different from ours?"

Anupam tried to say something in reply but the words got stuck in his throat and he was unable to reply or utter a word.

"It's all due to your foolishness...and your stupid assumption that this generation is different from ours!"

Anupam walked the rest of the way in silence. He felt like a criminal. And he felt responsible for the entire episode. It was he who had stuck a thorn within the innocent, unsuspecting heart of a young boy. After returning home, Anupam stood outside the door of Bappa's room in total silence. It seemed to him that his own heart had stopped beating all of a sudden. He did not dare to switch on the light. But he could hear the sound of muffled sobs within the room. His own heart turned over in pain as he heard it. He turned back to find Anita looking at him. But she turned her face away as soon as he looked at her. But Anupam could see the tears in Anita's eyes and turned away his own face.

There was just one day in between. One day before Ranen and his family left the place. This sylvan world—Musabani-Rakha-Haludpukur—had never seemed so insipid to Anupam before. The hills, the forests and the sky had suddenly become void of colour. In fact, all the colours seemed to have vanished from the entire locality. The breeze merely carried the odour of copper and had totally lost its healing touch. There was nothing soft or gentle in anything here. This day in between seemed like the dusty page of a book which Anupam turned without any enthusiasm. Anita had said, "Bappa, why don't you go out for a walk?"

Bappa had not replied. But his eyes seemed to say, "I have nowhere to go. All I can do is return home."

The morning passed and melted into evening and then, finally night.

Anjali was going away! Going away for good!

As soon as Anupam woke up the next morning he remembered that Anjali and her family would be leaving that day.

Anjali, twenty years ago I would think of you the moment I woke up in the morning, just like I am remembering you today. I could see your face in my mind's eye and I would go out and stand on the balcony for a glimpse of you. Then I heard the sound of a door opening and I saw you walking out of your room with your books. You would lift your eyes and look at me. That look would stay with me the whole day.

"Anjali and her family are leaving this morning," Anupam could not bring himself to utter these words without thinking of Bappa. Anjali, Ranen and Jhumjhum were forbidden words now, not meant to be spoken aloud. They were like the pebbles used in a catapult which were meant to hurt innocent victims. The way he remembered seeing a Santhal boy kill an innocent bird with his catapult for no rhyme or reason!

Anupam washed his face and brushed his teeth but did not know what to do next. Again he walked towards Bappa's room and stood at the door. Bappa was sitting on the bed, his face covered with both his hands. Anupam knew that he had not slept a wink the previous night. Anupam stood outside silently. He knew that Bappa's eyes—so like two gleaming silver cups—were brimming over with tears and that his slightest word of consolation would make them spill over. He said to himself: *Bappa, I can understand the age you belong to so well. The little bird fluttering within your heart is also mine. It is the same little bird that lived within my own heart when I was eighteen. Your generation has not changed, Bappa. Only your outer shell has changed. Deep inside your heart you are exactly what I was myself at eighteen.*

All through the colourless day Anupam had lived in the expectation that Jhumjhum would turn up suddenly and call out to Bappa as usual. She would shout and say, "We are leaving, Bappa. Won't you come to the station to see us off?" But, no. Jhumjhum had not come. Anupam wanted to tell Bappa, "Please go to the station and meet her, Bappa." Anupam could not forget Anita's accusing voice saying, "See what you've done! You had said that this generation is different." Her words had pierced his heart like a sharp arrow.

Anjali, you too had made the same mistake as me. Perhaps we both wanted to live life afresh through Bappa and Jhumjhum. Perhaps we wanted to make a gift of our lost moments of happiness to the young pair.

Anupam grew pensive for a moment. Perhaps he was thinking of Anjali. Or maybe he was thinking of Jhumjhum. They were both leaving the place. Going away…for good. Anjali had lived clinging on to Anupam's memories for twenty years. But she had left behind nothing but the memory of a few moments of physical proximity of one dark afternoon for Anupam. And also several moments of pride, enough to lighten the dark moments of his life as long as he lived. Anupam wanted nothing more from her. The only realisation that stood out was the fact that that they were leaving. Going away forever by the 9.15 train. The train did not stop here for long. No train stopped at any station for long. It merely picked up passengers in its many compartments of memories and moved on.

Anjali, you are trapped within a room right now. Your train no longer has any compartment of memories. Anjali, you refused to understand either Jhumjhum or Bappa. Being trapped within a room yourself, you merely wanted to look at the balcony outside. But those two were standing on the balcony itself from where they could see the open, endless sky.

"I think I'll go to the station once this morning," Anupam told Anita quite casually. "They are leaving this morning. I'd better go and see them off." His voice sounded somewhat rough. Anita did not reply.

The morning of their departure was bitterly cold once again. Anupam got ready and then wrapped a warm shawl around himself. As he stepped out, he saw a film of mist on the hilltop in the distance. A faint golden streak of sunlight shone through the mist and rested upon the treetops in the forest. The station was quite far from his guest house. Anupam walked at a brisk pace as he remembered that the train was at 9.15. He was afraid, really afraid of being too late.

Before long, he passed the Nawab Bari with its huge garden aglow with red roses. Anupam stopped short breathlessly at the sight. The entire garden seemed to be made up of a huge mass of red roses. Roses, roses everywhere! Red roses spread out like a bed! Anupam stopped and stared at the garden for a while.

I had sent you a bouquet of roses when you were awarded your PhD. But I had not put my name on the card. I had merely written, "From one who is the happiest person today."'.

Anupam opened the gate and got inside the garden. Then he picked up an armful of red roses and made a huge bouquet, tying it up with a creeper. Then he resumed his brisk walk, carrying the bouquet, feeling apprehensive about being too late and missing them altogether.

As Anupam approached the station, he saw them standing in a corner of the lonely platform. Anjali, Ranen and Jhumjhum. He also saw Bipin smoking a *bidi* in another corner some distance away. Their luggage was heaped nearby. Ranen saw Anupam and waved at him. Then he came forward and said, "I'm going in to buy the tickets. Be back soon." Anjali saw Anupam at a distance and her face lit up. She was looking exhausted but Anupam's presence brought on a soft radiance on her face. Jhumjhum ran to Anupam as she saw him coming. She touched his feet in salutation but could not bring herself to smile. Anupam gave her the bouquet of red roses, saying, "Bappa sent this bouquet for you, Jhumjhum."

"Bappa sent it for me? Really, Uncle?" Jhumjhum clasped the bouquet to her heart with both arms, holding it tight while taking in the scent. Her face lit up with a smile of pure joy. Anupam said, "He could not come himself because he is very ill."

Jhumjhum's face fell and she looked the picture of misery. Then she closed her eyes and smelled the roses again. Anupam walked towards Anjali.

"So you did come?" said Anjali. "I was sure that you wouldn't."

Anjali looked at the bouquet in Jhumjhum's arms and then looked deep into Anupam's eyes. She felt as though he had actually gifted the bouquet to Anjali herself. Anjali was at a loss for words. Then she suddenly said, "I had planned to give you something but I couldn't manage to buy anything."

"You have already given me a gift," said Anupam. "The memory of our days here."

Anjali gave Anupam a tragic look. She could not tell him that she had lost her memories for good and that she was leaving them behind her forever, here, among these woods. The memories she had been clinging on to for the last twenty years were lost completely. Never to be retrieved!

They could now hear the whistle of the train. Ranen was already back with the tickets. The whistle blew in a continuous blast as it echoed within the hearts of Anupam, Anjali and Jhumjhum. It seemed to be neverending. Finally the train rolled in and halted at the station. Ranen selected a compartment and Bipin put in their luggage there. Anjali and Jhumjhum got in quickly as the train did not stop here for long. No train stopped at any station for long!

The train was moving now…going far and yet further. There were faces in every window but Anupam had eyes for just two of them. One of them framed Anjali's face, looking at him with sorrowful eyes. The other framed Jhumjhum's, who was waving at him. As the train picked up speed, the two faces blended into one and he could only see Jhumjhum's seventeen-year-old face. Finally, the train itself was reduced to a mere dot before vanishing from his sight forever.

Anupam turned back and started walking briskly. He passed by the ticket counter and walked towards the distant signal and the railway track. Then he came to a sudden halt and looked away in the distance where the railway platform ended and the cactus bushes began. A shiver swept through his entire being as he saw Bappa. Bappa was standing there steadily gazing at the receding train, his eyes fixed on the distant horizon.